ALEXANDRIAN SUMMER

YITZHAK GORMEZANO GOREN

Translated by
YARDENNE GREENSPAN

Introduction by
ANDRÉ ACIMAN

NEW VESSEL PRESS
NEW YORK

ALEXANDRIAN SUMMER

New Vessel Press

www.newvesselpress.com

First published in Hebrew in 1978 as *Kayits Alexandroni*
Copyright © 2015 Yitzhak Gormezano Goren
Translation Copyright © 2015 New Vessel Press
Introduction Copyright © 2015 André Aciman

Published by arrangement with
The Institute for the Translation of Hebrew Literature

The author would like to express gratitude to Charline Spektor.

Library of Congress Cataloging-in-Publication Data
Goren, Yitzhak Gormezano
[Kayits Alexandroni. English]
Alexandrian Summer/ Yitzhak Gormezano Goren; translation by Yardenne Greenspan.
p. cm.
ISBN 978-1-939931-20-7
Library of Congress Control Number 2014921051
        I. Israel -- Fiction

"And to every people after their language"
Book of Esther I : 22

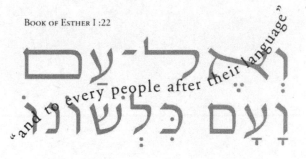

BOOK OF ESTHER I :22

Published with the support of the
Institute for the Translation of Hebrew Literature, Israel
and the Cultural Department of the Consulate
of Israel, New York

Introduction

ON DECEMBER 21, 1951, YITZHAK GORMEZANO GOREN, aged ten and accompanied by his parents, left his home on Rue Delta in Alexandria to rejoin his two brothers who had already moved to Israel. That the whole family decided to leave Egypt as early as 1951 shows that they had the uncanny prescience to read the writing on the wall long before most Egyptian Jews realized that their days in the country were numbered.

The military coup that was to overthrow King Farouk in 1952 and, with his ouster, eventually dissolve all remnants of multi-national life in Egypt, can only confirm the Gormezano Gorens' sense that life as they'd known it in Alexandria was fast coming to an end. Surging anti-Western and anti-Semitic rhetoric on the streets and in radio broadcasts had turned Egypt into a tinderbox that was to explode with the Suez Canal War of 1956, a war that proved disastrous to Egypt's European community. French and British nationals were instantly expelled, their exodus immediately followed by the expulsion of the majority of Egypt's 85,000 Jews, most of whose ancestors had been living along the Nile and its Delta for more than a millennium and long before the advent of Islam.

Alexandrian Summer is a nostalgic, farewell portrait of a world that was fast expiring but still refused to see that history had written it off. The outward signs were deceptive enough to placate everyone's worst fears: money, beaches, tennis, races, gambling, servants, friends, visits, outings, sugary delights; the whole fabric of day-to-day life smoothed over by that invigorating source of nattering called gossip, guile, and more gossip.

This, after all, was a multi-ethnic, multi-religious, multi-sexual, multi-everything society where Copt, Jew, Muslim, Catholic, and Greek Orthodox lived tolerably well together and where multilingualism was the order of the day. Everyone was part Levantine, part European, part Egyptian, and one hundred percent hodgepodge, just as everyone's sentences were spiced with words and expressions lifted from French, Italian, Arabic, Ladino, Turkish, Greek, English, and whatever else came by. Tart-to-toxic *bons mots* in a mix of six to eight languages could singe you just enough to shake you up but without causing any damage. Similarly, the mix of populations was never perfect, and cultures and creeds jostled one another without scruple. There again, the tussling was amicable enough and never deadly. But no one was fooled for long. The peaceful coexistence of so many creeds and nationalities may have been asking too much of mankind and in the end was too good to be true. It never lasts; it never did.

But this is still summer, and as happens every year, hordes of Cairenes would descend upon Alexandria to summer there. The host family and their guest family go back years together. The son of one family is a jockey who hopes to win on the racetrack, while the daughter of the other family asks him to choose between her and horses. She tempts him at the beach with her body, but the young man resists, only to end up being taken to a brothel by his father. Meanwhile, his younger brother is a compulsive sex machine who'll undress for any boy who so much as cuddles up to him. There are many more characters, each one, in the end, destined to spar with the other, even when there's something like love or not quite love between them. Nothing is ever perfect. In the end nothing could patch up the billowy screen that unbeknownst to everyone was fast being ripped apart.

Things could get worse. When a Jewish jockey wins

the summer's race against a Muslim, a virulent fever of anti-Semitism erupts upon the city, and Alexandria is almost ready to burst into flames. Anti-Semitism is brutal and ugly, but Gormezano Goren is by no means unaware that the contemptuous treatment of Arabs, particularly of Arab servants in Jewish and European households, is no less disquieting a harbinger of Muslim unrest and rage. A servant should never stop to think that a Jewish boy's toy train could cost seven times what he earns to feed his kids each month.

This striking example highlights Gormezano Goren's light touch whenever seeking to convey the resentment and bitterness forever brewing beneath the surface in Muslim-Jewish relations. In another passage, he nimbly demonstrates how combustible were the dealings between both groups by showing what happens when an Egyptian jockey accuses his Jewish competitor of drugging his racehorse. Mass hysteria could easily erupt. These are small, incidental observations but they speak volumes. Ultimately, in a world being scuttled far too quickly for anyone to gauge the extent of the damaged relations between Arabs and Jews, Gormezano Goren's words are as prophetic as they are disturbing: "Times have changed, and Jews have changed."

Alexandrian Summer is not so much the story of a peculiar culture or of a particular class or even of a specific moment in history. It is the story of what could only be called a "way of life"—an altogether unquantifiable and elusive term that conveys only a fraction of what life was like for the Jews of Egypt. Every day was lived as if it were the last. What came after Egypt was fantasy and fear.

I knew that way of life well. I was born into it on the very year Yitzhak left Alexandria. That way of life lasted another fifteen years until my Jewish family too was expelled from Egypt. I knew the beaches, I knew the taste of special foods, I knew the scent of clothes drying in the sun. And I knew Rue Delta, since I too lived on that street. It is on Rue Delta that I spent my last night in Alexandria. Our house, like the Gormezano Gorens', was located midway between the beach and the racetrack. I too have watched the races and walked from the races to the beach and from the beach to the races.

In my long years away, I have met others who had lived on Rue Delta. I have even met someone whom I did not know in Alexandria but with whom it came as a total surprise to discover that the two of us had grown up in the identical building. At first, I found it hard to believe, and in the café where we met that first time, I asked her to map out the layout of her parents' apartment on a paper napkin. Hers seemed totally wrong. It couldn't possibly have been the same building. But then it suddenly hit me that she was not wrong at all; her apartment was identical to ours except that hers had the exact, but reverse layout. What luck, I thought. Everything seemed settled ... except for a round room. I asked her if her apartment had a round room in the back. No, theirs didn't have such a room. But then she thought about it, gave out a sudden cry, and had an epiphany. Yes, theirs did have a round room and she knew its precise spot. It was just that she hadn't thought of that room in over sixty years! No one used that room, no one lived in it. In both our cases it had become a storage, bric-a-brac space. And as we described that room to each other, we could almost make out the moldy, woody smell of the space, which in her family's, as in ours, was the last stop for dead chairs and defunct cabinets and chests of drawers.

Alexandrian Summer is a return to a mythical past, to a lost paradise that was not really a paradise but that, being lost, has, over the years, acquired all the makings of one. One's childhood is always yearned for, and this is young Yitzhak's—or Robert, as he is called in the book—paradise.

I still remember our last year in Alexandria. By then, our assets had been frozen and my father's factory nationalized, and even our cars were no longer ours, though we were allowed to drive them. Our days were numbered, and we knew it.

Or did we? My father claimed that he would have remained in Egypt even without an income. Come to think of it I myself could not even conceive of a life outside Egypt. Our living room and in the end even the round room in the back were packed with suitcases, and still all of us were convinced this was all for show, as if by going through the motions of packing and pretending we were indeed leaving, we were merely placating a hostile deity who would, at the last instant, spare us the final leave taking and tell us it was all a test, just a test. We were never going away.

Ironically, that final year is the one I remember best, because it was the most tumultuous. I remember my grandmother and her sister, my great aunt, and I remember the bickering with neighbors and the tussles with my brother and the fights between my parents, and the loud screams when our servants fought with those of our neighbors; everyone's temper was volcanic that year, because it was clear that things were falling apart and that we were on our last legs and still couldn't believe that the end was near.

But I remember Saturdays. We weren't religious, though I recall my great aunt turning on the radio loud on Saturday mornings to hear songs in both Yiddish and Ladino. She preferred the Ashkenazi songs and prayers, and to the sound of these songs I remember she would start preparing for Saturday's lunch, because there were always guests on Saturdays. And even if we didn't exaggerate the Sabbath spirit, still there was a festive air about the household, and our cook Abdou, who spoke Ladino, would put on his cleanest outfit and utter those few words in Hebrew that he knew far better than I did. In Gormez-ano Goren's own words, "A pleasant breeze blew from the sea. The tumult of bathers sounded from afar: Muslims, Christians, and Jews desecrating the Sabbath. On the street, cars honked hysterically. The entire city rumbled and roared, and nevertheless a Sabbath serenity was felt all around."

Every Alexandrian remembers this way of life and knows it is forever lost. At the very least, *Alexandrian Summer* gives us one final, splendid season in this mythi-cal metropolis.

André Aciman

To my brother Haim-Victor
who was born in Alexandria,
immigrated to Israel,
lived most of his life in the United States
and considered himself a citizen of the world

ALEXANDRIAN SUMMER

1. From Twenty Years Away

The Sporting Club neighborhood, the horse racing tracks beyond the tramlines. At the intersection of Rue Delta and the Corniche, by the sea, stands house number twenty-four, all seven of its stories (we used to climb up to the flat roof and shoot paper arrows down at the industrious ants running around on the sidewalk, back and forth, as if there were purpose to all this frenzy).

An Arab doorman, Badri, stands guard, squinting at the sun. His face is tan and emaciated. His little boy, Abdu, loiters at his side, helping him watch the shadows stretching over the sidewalk and the passing cars, headed toward the sea. Badri and his son welcome anyone approaching the building with an alert greeting, "*Ahalan, ya sidi,*" full of expectation: Will the guest give *bakshish* or not? If the guest does tip them, they escort him with bows all the way to the elevator door. If he doesn't—they point lazily in the direction of the moldy duskiness.

The elevator is ancient, barred with black metal and faded gold openwork and bitten by reddish rust. The door slams with a metallic shake, and … a miracle! The elevator rises with a buzz, dragging with effort a looping tail that grows longer as the elevator ascends. Chilling stories have been told about power outages between the fourth and fifth floors; fights between neighbors, beginning in the stairwell, intensified in the gloom of the elevator, later to dissipate outside, in the subtropical sun that ridicules all human endeavors.

Second floor, that's as far as I go. If you aren't lazy, you could climb it by foot. A copper plate bearing the name of a Jewish family, descendants of Sephardic Jews from the era of the Spanish Expulsion (their last name is the name of their hometown with the suffix "*ano*"). The doorbell rings. A dark-haired and skinny servant opens the door and addresses you in lilting Mediterranean French: "*Oui, missier, quisqui voulez?*" and you stutter and ask: "Is this where Robert … *Robby* lives?"

The servant is surprised that a thirty-year-old man is interested in a ten-year-old boy, but he does not voice his opinion as long as he isn't asked to. "Robby—there!" He signals toward the balcony, at the far end of the apartment. "Should I call him?"

"No, no! Please, there's no need."

The Arab servant looks at you with a hint of suspicion. "Who you, *missier*?" and you give him your name, Hebraized to fit Israel of the 1950s, which rejected all foreign sounds. The servant does not decipher any connection between the two names. To him the strange name could be Greek or Turkish or Italian or Maltese or Armenian or French or British or even American. Alexandria is the center of the world, a cosmopolitan city. You want to add: yes, I used to be Robert, too. Twenty years ago. I'm coming from twenty years away. I won't interrupt, I just want to watch. I won't interfere, God forbid. No one will notice me. I just want to tell the story of one summer, a Mediterranean summer, an Alexandrian summer.

2. A Family from Cairo

Waves of memories of that city—Alexandria—rise and recede. The story of the Alexandrian summer does not present itself easily. It is wrapped in layers of nostalgia, of oblivion, of generalizations. I search for the objective, the distinguishing. Should I tell it in first or third person? Should I use real names or give my characters aliases, adding a note along the lines of "any resemblance to real persons is purely incidental"? These may be small details, but they are the ones holding back my pen.

I want to tell you about the Hamdi-Ali family. What is it like, really, this family? The Hamdi-Ali family embodies *joie de vivre*, the unending Mediterranean energy. Yes, Mediterranean. And maybe it's because of this Mediterranean-ness that I'm sitting here, telling this story. Here, in Israel, which feels much more like Eastern Europe to me. I might as well be sitting on the shore of the Baltic Sea, for all the distance I feel from the Mediterranean, which can be seen from my window in Tel Aviv. That's why I am eager to tell the story of the Hamdi-Alis, and the story of Alexandria. A Jewish family from Cairo that came to Alexandria to spend a summer of joy. Alexandria of the days of King Farouk, with his hook-mustache and his dark glasses, the Alexandria I knew as a child, this Alexandria, which has been feeding my imagination for over twenty years, from the day I left it on December 21st, 1951, when I was ten years old.

A storm brewed as we sailed from the port toward the lighthouse, and didn't stop until we reached the shores of Italy. There, we were welcomed by Christmas snow. Winter was at its peak, but me, I wish to tell the story of a summer, a summer in Alexandria, an Alexandrian summer: vacation, horse races, sailboats, fishing for sea urchins, swallowing crabs, platonic (and not so platonic) romances, traffic jams, traffic jams, traffic jams, honking, honking, honking of cars and cars and more cars. All rushing toward the Corniche, the busy road overlooking the sea, where vacationers at the beach rented shacks so they wouldn't be forced to undress in the public dressing rooms with "all those Arabs."

3. The Royal Family

Car. Car. Truck. Motorcycle. Another car. Yes, he made it! He got it down. Next: no point in listing a bicycle. Another motorcycle. Yes ... it's hard to see the license plate number from the balcony—but he has it down! What a beauty— there's a luxury car. Quick, write down the number. DeSoto, Chrysler, Lincoln Continental. When they approach the intersection they are forced to slow down and then he can write down their numbers. And if there's a traffic jam he can even rest for a few seconds. What a festival of sounds!

"The summer in Alexandria is a nightmare!"

"I don't understand, why aren't drivers forbidden from honking in urban areas? Don't give me that look. In any civilized city in the world ..."

"What a cacophony! I'm about to lose my mind."

"If you think Cairo's any better, my dear, you're mistaken, *ma chère*. When you approach the Qasr-al-Nil Bridge, the honking can even wake up the Pharaohs in their tombs!"

"Yes, but in Paris ..."

"And in London ..."

Those grownups! Living in Alexandria. Most of them born there. Arabic? God forbid! French, sometimes English. Looking askance with coquettish flirtation at the fashion hubs of Europe, making a commendable effort not to lag behind the *dernier cri* from Paris, London or New York. Especially the women, as they sit around playing rummy. Robby often eavesdrops on their conversations. He's the youngest, much younger than his older siblings. Mostly solitary. No, not a tragic loneliness of the kind that gives birth to reclusive poets—nonsense, he has friends his age. But he can't spend all day at their houses or have them over at his. In Alexandria, middle class children do not play in the street, heaven forbid.

And so he invents all sorts of strange games.

"Well, boys, is your mission clear? Whenever a car passes, you take down its license plate number. Look alive, boys, stay on your toes. If you notice any suspicious movement, report to headquarters immediately! Okay, at ease!" Perhaps these orders were spoken in some Hollywood film he saw in one of the theaters on Boulevard Ramleh? Or perhaps he just made up some sort of rationale for his bizarre obsession with taking down the license plate numbers of passing cars?

"What are you writing-writing-writing down there in your notebook all-the-time-all-the-time, Robby?"

"I'm, uh ..."

"And most importantly boys, maintain secrecy! Never reveal your mission."

"Uh, uh, I'm not writing, I-I-I'm ... uh ... drawing."

"Oh, Livia, you have to see Robby's drawings, a real talent. When he grows up, he'll be an architect. Robby, come show Madame Livia your drawings."

"Later ... later ... I'm, uh, busy right now."

"He's busy. He's busy. *He's busy!*" They laugh among themselves. Not even ten yet, and he's busy! Does he shop at the Hanneaux department stores, like us? No. Does he play cards, *en-matinée*, like us? No. Must he rebuke the servants from time to time, like us? No. Then what is he so busy with? "It's your turn, Geena darling."

"Thank you."

Writing down and cataloging cars—that is a task for summer days. In winter: a raging wind, rain, hail, school. The balconies in Alexandria are open. No shutters and no blinds. The apartments are sprawling and no one is in need of an extra room, and so the balcony is a balcony, open to the gale that revolts in winter, and to the rays of sun, searing and burning in summer. They say you can bake a pita on the stones of the pyramids. But Alex is cool and temperate. Reminiscent of ...

"What are you talking about? Capri! Really! How can

you even compare them?"

"Who can afford to go to Capri or the Riviera every year?"

"That's why they all come surging here in the summer."

A 1940 Topolino. The screeching of the brakes. A belch, a hiccup, a moan, pulling up, right below the balcony. Robby doesn't even get a chance to take its number down. Three cars pull up behind it. Three next to it. Another traffic jam! Curses in all the languages of the Mediterranean. No one can compete with the Greeks for a good swear word! And honking, honking in all scales.

David Hamdi-Ali, tall as a toreador, blond as a Nordic cavalier, elegant like Rudolph Valentino, leaps with agility in his supple white leather shoes, subduing the drowsy virus whose journey through his body has finally run its course to conclude with a series of asthmatic coughs. David ignores the swearing and the cursing, and even responds to the threats with Olympian serenity. How can they know that, on top of everything else, he's also a "dirty Jew?" He opens the car door for his mother, Emilie, with a light bow, expressing his love and adoration. From the moment her feet touch the sidewalk, he ignores the other passengers, his father Joseph and his brother Victor. The eleven-year-old boy filters out, looking around with suspicious, coveting eyes, fixing his gaze on all passing women, with no regard to age or race. Before he even knows which way is up, he receives a blow to the back of the neck, his brother hissing at him: "Stand up straight, moron!" This is simply the nature of things: David was born a prince, and he won't tolerate his brother, with his infuriating habit of sticking out his neck and rolling his watery eyes, ruining the image of his family. Victor, just like his big brother, is wearing a white summer suit, but on him it looks like a tattered sack. It is strewn with wrinkles in back and filthy in the front, like the face of an old Arab woman from a forgotten village. David drove the Topolino for more than six hours in the blazing summer heat, yet he emerges from the car ironed and spotless. You're born this way. Emilie adjusts the fluttery white net that slides down her wide-brimmed hat—an entirely superfluous gesture, seeing as how the net had already been sloping at a natural, graceful, elegant angle. You are either born a queen, or you are not born a queen. Joseph wears a wine-colored fez which seems too big for his head even though it is not. His clothes also seem to hang on his body. Some souls are at home in the world, while other souls … Joseph sighs and shakes his head, and the red fringe of the fez swings with each shake.

Stretching their bones. Six hours in that Topolino … It's a wonder it didn't break down in the middle of the desert. David drives it as if it were nothing less than a Rolls-Royce, but one has to admit it's slightly less comfortable than that. Ahhhh … what a wonderful breeze from the sea! This is Alexandria! There, that's the apartment, on the second floor, you see, Victor? Victor, stand up straight, you idiot! That kid over there, that's Robby. You'll be friends! Waving. Yes, Robby answers with a wave and disappears from the balcony, running to announce to his parents: "The Hamdi-Alis are here! The Hamdi-Alis are here!"

Salem, the servant, is sent down to help carry their luggage. Robby trails behind him. The notebook remains on the wall of the balcony. The wind flips through the pages, not understanding the meaning of all these numbers, numbers and more numbers.

4. Servants

Surrounded by water. Water, water, water. In the north, her full breasts dip in the water of the Mediterranean. In the south, the waves of Lake Mariout cool her behind with arousing caresses. In the east, her fingers flutter through the Nile as it runs its brown water with limp sleepiness. In the west, the sea of sand that is the Libyan Desert sends waves of hot breath onto Alexandria's burning back, feverish with desire. Alexandria. Alex. Sea. Delta. Desert.

"I haaaaate the desert!"

"It's stifling, and it's so local. Oh, a picnic on the snowy Alps, in the dense forests of Europe … Oh, Christmas in Paris!"

"When have you ever been to France, Annette?"

"I haven't, but I went to school at the *Lycée français*."

City dwellers. Wild nature? Only in Hollywood movies. The Nile? Too filthy, swarming with Arabs. Sunrise in the desert? Leave that to Lawrence of Arabia, he likes that kind of thing, poor devil. The pyramids? Yes, they're all right. At any rate, they're close to Cairo. You can visit them in the morning and then arrange a game of rummy with some friends in Heliopolis. And all the American tourists are crazy about the pyramids, which is saying something, isn't it? But going all the way to Luxor? Just to see some stones? With all due respect to the temples of Karnak, spending the night there, at the end of the world, among the Arabs, away from civilization? Please.

Yes, that is what they're like, cosmopolitan to the bone. Speaking to one another in French, English, Spanish, Italian, Greek. They know only the Arabic they absolutely need. Most of the servants speak French, and they are the go-betweens connecting their masters to the locals.

Those who grew up in Israel of the 1950s, in the lap of progressive socialism, the brotherhood of man, the equality of races—at least in theory—must now be chuckling with patronizing contempt; they must find it difficult to understand how cultivated people accepted such backward colonial feudalism. True, Alexandria was rotten to the core, but its rot had roots, was saturated in history. Dig deep through the muck and you'll find the remnants of a crumbling papyrus, or a lock of hair from the shrunken head of a mummy. Something is rotten, truly rotten, in the kingdom of Alexandria. That's why I love her so much, Alexandria. A city that lets you live like a carefree lord without even being rich. Of course, you had to be European, or at least Jewish, and of minimal intelligence, and even that wasn't always a staunch demand. Money? Money was meant to be wasted on pleasures and reveling. Only misers save up for a rainy day. Balls, trips, sailing, racing and card games. You earn between thirty and a hundred pounds per month. You pay four-and-a-half for rent and live in a castle, surrounded by servants, each living on two pounds per month. What a glorious gap! And in fact you are nothing more than a pathetic petit bourgeois. In Europe you would have tightened your purse strings just to get through the month debt-free. All day long, your wife would scrub the floors of the sorry little studio apartment you were able to afford in paradisaical Paris or legendary London. But here, in Alex, Monsieur No-Name easily keeps two slaves working for and worshipping him. You can't be a nobody if you have two servants, male and female, living and toiling in your home twenty-four hours a day, six-and-a-half days a week (on their half-day off they go to their miserable villages to see their sick parents and their lice-infected little siblings) — all for four Egyptian pounds, two-and-a-half for the men, one-and-a-half for the women.

"They don't deserve any more than that!"

"They're so lazy!"

"The worst is when you have a pair of lovebirds on your hands. God help us!"

"He pesters her all day long, and who does she complain to? You, of course. Worse than children."

"And the women aren't *sainte-ni-touche* either."

"And when they start eating for two—what a nightmare!"

"I had a Bedouin female servant once. Green eyes *this*

big. Then we hired a Sudanese man, black as tar. One day they were cleaning the bathroom together. Don't ask. Suddenly I heard cries like a woman giving birth. I ran over but the door was locked. I yelled for my husband, Isidore, and he went to get the doorman, and together we broke the door down. What did we find? Don't ask! The two of them ... I'm too embarrassed to even hint at the state we found them in. She, the poor thing, her clothes all torn, lying in the bathtub, almost passed out. And he, naked and black, beating her to death. She must have refused him ..."

"Horrible!"

"And that's nothing. You know my aunt Fortunée, right? My mother's sister. Once she was alone at home and asked her servant, his name was Ahmed, if I'm not mistaken ..."

"They're all called Ahmed."

"At any rate, she asked him to go down and pick up her husband's suit from the cleaner's. He said, 'I won't budge until you sleep with me!'"

"Nooooo!"

"What do you mean, no? She told me herself. But you know Fortunée, she doesn't scare so easy ..."

"I would have died right on the spot."

"All calm and collected, she tells him: 'Fine, why not? An attractive guy like you! Wait for me here, I'll go prepare myself.' The Don Juan was so confident of his conquest that he wasn't even careful. She ran downstairs, to call the doorman. And meanwhile, he prepared himself ..."—the first, hesitant purrs of laughter are sounded among the ladies—"and when they came upstairs, she and the doorman, they found him ready. Ha ha ha!" The solitary purrs join in to form a light, steady bellowing, still uneasy. But embarrassment slowly evaporates. Now the laughter is mischievous, envisioning. In a moment it will become enormous, wild, somewhat sick. Victorian society in Alex binds itself by the webs of convention, and so the slightest hint of lechery gives way to emotions and urges buried deep under the blanket of appearances. It's hard to imagine that any of these respectable ladies went so far as to imagine the proud organ of the brash black man, but even that is not out of the question. And if we may, for a moment, part from the narrow and strict realm of facts and amuse ourselves with conjectures, I would suspect the elegant, snobbish, quasi-aristocratic Madame Livia (there are no real aristocrats in Alexandria). And how can we know what goes on in the minds of matrons in their forties, with their spotless reputations? In any case, she is the one now calling her friends to order, reminding them assertively that they did not convene here in order to gossip, but for a serious, respectable endeavor—the game of rummy. Please, Geena, it's your turn to shuffle!

5. Emilie

The small commotion raised by the royal family continues at the curb. With movements worthy of Nijinsky, calculated to the smallest detail and leaving luminous traces in the air, David twirls around the sleeping Beetle, pulling out another suitcase and another briefcase and another brown-paper package, like a magician pulling a rabbit from his hat. He piles everything on the sidewalk in a lovely mess, almost a work of art. His brother, Victor, sits down on one of the suitcases, urging it to gallop up the street with wild yelps, but a precise slap to the back of his shorn neck throws him right off his steed, and he almost crashes into Robby, who trails after Salem the servant and Abdu, the doorman's son. They had come outside to carry the Hamdi-Alis' luggage. The quickness of the two little Arabs and the ingratiating looks in their eyes insinuate great hopes of generous bakshish from the *sidi*'s hands.

All the while, Madame Emilie is busy touching up her makeup. The side mirror of the car reflects her full face, still preserving a smidgeon of its youthful blush.

"What are you talking about? Emilie Hamdi-Ali used to be a beauty!" Grandma says knowingly. "When she married Joseph Hamdi-Ali, everyone was shocked. Rich? No. Handsome? No. And no smarter than anyone else ..."

"Perhaps neither smart nor handsome," Renée Marika chimes in, "but rich, he was. And how! That's why Emilie married him," she added maliciously.

"No," Grandma insists. "He only got rich later, when he started with the horse races. When they got married he was a mere stock market clerk. They barely made a living. I remember it as if it were yesterday. They lived next door to us, in Moharram Bey. One morning he got up and went to Cairo and came back a joker ..."

All the women burst out laughing, and Grandma doesn't understand what she did wrong. Her daughter comes to her aid: "Jockey, Mama, not joker!"

Madame Marika quickly concludes, "She wanted to say jockey, but she saw the joker winking at her between her cards."

But Grandma denies such luck in her game: "The joker only goes to the young ones," she whines.

Once the laughter dies down, Madame Marika adds secretively: "When I was in Cairo recently, there was a rumor going around in Heliopolis that Joseph Hamdi-Ali is actually ..." she pauses for a moment, her gaze flitting over her friends' faces, preparing to land and sting: "Turkish! And his real name is Yoossoof!"

A real scoop. General shock. Gaping eyes and mouths. Heads nodding and shaking in agreement, in denial, in disbelief. She must soften her target: "They say he converted to Judaism just for Emilie, because her father, Davidshon, wouldn't give her to a Muslim!" Madame Marika is certain this discovery will eliminate whatever remained of Emilie Hamdi-Ali's reputation.

But Grandma spoils it all, saying in her conniving innocence: "How lovely! He gave up his faith and converted for her. Oh, love, love. Nothing in the world can stand in its path. Not religion, not parents ... nothing!"

A dire thought passes through Madame Marika's mind: Vita, her husband, would not have sacrificed so much for her. Love! Ha! With rage and pain she remembers the businesslike efficiency that characterized her marriage. Love? What's love? Nonsense. She expects support from the other women, someone to speak ill of Emilie, to find fault in her marriage to a proselyte, but her wish slams against a fortified wall of dreamy eyes. They are all giving in to their own reminiscing.

And as if to make matters worse, Grandma sighs, "He calls her '*la bella donna*.'"

Blood pounds against Madame Marika's temples, and she orders them to carry on with the game. Go on, shuffle ... shuffle the cards!

"Her older son, David, is also quite a man," Grandma starts, but her friend Marika's angry look paralyzes her tongue and she focuses on her cards with the gravity worthy of a game of rummy among matrons, in the early afternoon of a sunny summer's day in Alexandria.

6. DAVID

David Hamdi-Ali, Joseph Hamdi-Ali's eldest son, is one of the stars of the racetrack in Egypt. His rating on the jockey exchange, "the slave market," as he calls it jokingly, is one of the highest. He maintains a strict regime, stubbornly fighting against the tendency to gain weight that he inherited from his mother, which might put his career in jeopardy. His diet gives him a film star's figure. He is thin, tall and elegant, adored by all girls. It seems he need do nothing more than stretch out an agile, muscular arm and pluck from the garden: Rose, Marguerite, Hortense, Lilly … But Hamdi-Ali the son looks to Robby's sister, of all girls, and she is one of an insignificant minority who does not fantasize about the racing cavalier. Here we have a seeming background for a tragedy, or at least for a melodrama of unrequited love. But no. Though we can surely say that his love for her is genuine, we cannot say it is wild beyond all common sense, and certainly not as strong as death. Moreover, though we can certainly say that in her heart of hearts she feels completely indifferent toward him, she hasn't bothered to shake him off with a clearcut rejection. And so this lukewarm romance continues to provide fodder for thought and gossip for Grandma's card club friends.

"You know," Grandma tells Robby's mother, "that David Hamdi-Ali doesn't seem bad at all."

"What are you trying to say?"

"Nothing, nothing. Only that maybe we should put some pressure on your daughter … not let her act according to …"

"Mama, please! You know she's a big girl and she needs to make up her own mind. Her father is very adamant about this matter. He says we mustn't, under any circumstances, push her into the arms of a groom against her will."

"The way they did to me, my parents," Grandma identifies. "Your father, they made me …" But when she sees that her daughter shows no enthusiasm in speaking ill of her father, she returns to the original topic: "All right, then let her choose for herself, but have her choose already, and choose wisely! What does she think, that princess? That boys like David are just rolling around the street? Big and tall like a Turkish guard and blond and beautiful and educated." The further she enumerates David's virtues, the worse is her anger at her indifferent granddaughter, and finally she puts aside the pillowcase she is embroidering with demonstrative distaste (the pillowcase being a part of the dowry she and her daughter are preparing for Robby's sister), as if to say: Who am I working for? She'll remain an old maid, or marry some Greek Orthodox or Coptic Christian, or worse—an Arab, heaven forbid!

"She's still young!" says her daughter, who heard even what Grandma did not say, and quickly hands her back the pillowcase. Grandma exhales with contempt, takes the pillowcase, inserts a purl thread and returns to the intricate embroidery. Finally she relinquishes her displeasure with irrelevant questions, such as: "When will we finally get a letter from the boys in Israel?" or "Are the Murads planning on staying with us again this summer?"

She knows there is no clear answer to her first question. Robby's two older brothers had left for Israel a year before, and since then communication has been scarce. As for the second question, she is well aware of the answer: indeed, the Coptic Murads will spend the scalding summer in Alex. Madame Murad and her two daughters, the black-haired Thérèse and the blonde, braided Juliette, have already rented out the large living room, which will serve as their bedroom for the summer months. Mister Murad will join his family only on the weekends, unable to leave his business in Cairo unattended. Two of the remaining four rooms will be used by the Hamdi-Alis, and so Robby will have to spend nights in his parents' bedroom, which thrills him to no end.

7. VICTORICO

Happy is the black sheep who has never seen her dark reflection in a puddle—she does not perceive herself to be any different than her pearly white sisters as they step out from the pond. This is the case for eleven-year-old Victor: a sort of contemptible John Lackland, resembling a court jester's bastard more than a king's son. No wonder he views his brother's regal mannerisms with mercifulness mixed with a pinch of ridicule. He silently accepts the crowned prince's generous beatings, as if saying: beat on, beat on, but only I know what you're really worth, his pouting lips twisting into a crooked smile. He hardly speaks to his parents and brother, and among adults is considered quiet and almost slow. This misconception is enhanced by the appearance of his elongated head and his face, which resembles a horse's snout. Grandma's card club friends are sure there is a connection between Victorico's horse face and his father's dealings.

"He was probably thinking of a racing mare when he was ..." they giggle. This is an innocent comment in principle, but it paves the way to more bold variations: "Maybe Victorico really is the son of Joseph and ... Leila, the purebred that Joseph loved more than his own wife?"

Once laughter dies down some of the ladies express shock at the vulgar joke, but who can tighten the reins on a gossiping matron once her tongue is set loose? Madame Marika finally brings matters to their ultimate climax: "You're all mistaken. I know for a fact that Emilie is Victor's mother. It's Joseph who isn't his father." Here she grows silent. Curiosity bubbles. Some of the women suspect that she is pulling their leg, but most of them swallow the bait and cannot help but ask: "Then who is his father?"

Madame Marika puts on a mask of mystery and finally says, "A stallion!"

That's it. Unbridled excitement. They writhe with laughter, folding in half and balling up and nearly falling off their seats. Almost violently, they slap one another on the back of the arm. Tears run like water, and Madame Marika, finally celebrating victory, feels her underwear filling with sweet warmth, followed immediately by cool moisture. She runs to the bathroom, and the laughter goes on unrestrained.

That entire time the children, elsewhere, exchange impressions and experiences from the schools they go to during the dreary winter months. Suddenly they each become vehement patriots of their schools. From here the road carries directly to the eternal question: Which city is neater, Cairo or Alexandria? To Victor's argument that Cairo is the capital, Robby quips that Alexandria is the second largest port in the Mediterranean and the largest in the Middle East. And if, as Victor says, Cairo is larger and has more inhabitants, "Alex," Robby claims, "is more cultured!"

Victor protests bitterly, this is completely baseless, but Robby insists: "Besides, Alexandria has the sea, and what does Cairo have? Desert!"

"Pyramids! One of the seven wonders of the world!"

"And we have the lighthouse on Pharos Island, that's also one of the seven wonders!"

"But the lighthouse was destroyed and drowned!"

"If you have it so good, why do you spend the summer here? Who asked you to come?"

This cuts Victor's arguments short and he answers hypocritically, "It *is* really silly, but what can I do? My parents make me come here."

Robby looks at him with disbelief and sets him up, "Then let's run to the beach!"

"Let's!" Victor responds with an enthusiasm that negates his fabricated indifference toward Alexandria's charms. They step out of their pants and run around in their underwear, looking for bathing suits. On the way they are submerged by a deluge of rebukes from the grownups, and Victor collects a dry slap to the back of the head, but what dam can ever stop the raging Nile during the high tide of June?

At the doorway, Robby says, "See? If we were in Cairo we could only dream of the sea right now!"

They slam the door on the morality of grownups, who claim that it isn't nice to run down the street bare-foot, in their bathing suits, and that their feet are going to burn on the scalding asphalt, and that they shouldn't stay in the sun too long because they'll get overheated, and that they shouldn't go in the water right after eating because they'll have cramps, and that they should wipe themselves dry when they come out of the water, and that they shouldn't drink cold water or soda with ice cubes when they're sweating, and that, and that, and that ... They roll down the stairs, pushing each other, and their laughter echoes all through the building. Now that the threat of his brother is removed, Victor goes wild. Robby still behaves in a civilized manner. But when the door-man greets them with saccharine politeness, they stick out their tongue at him. The doorman's son quickly comes out to defend his father's honor, spitting an Arabic curse word at them, something to do with their mothers. Only after some time, in Israel, where this curse involving one's mother's reproductive organs would be integrated into Hebrew slang, Robby would be able to figure out the first part of the expression, as well. But they are too busy to mind some little Abdu, too preoccupied to try and punch him. Onward to the boardwalk, towels flapping and bare feet skipping over the scorching asphalt.

Robby thinks, how good it would be if I had a brother my age, like this Victor!

8. Kudjoocome

Siesta in Alexandria. An hour of siesta in the midst of an Alexandrian summer, a Mediterranean summer, a summer of the early 1950s. An hour in which everybody floats above ground, in which every word is uttered as a whisper, so as not to desecrate the serenity of the moment. Only the antique grandfather clock in the darkened hall keeps swinging its pendulum patiently, and every fifteen minutes it erupts in sounds from a faraway world, laden with yearning: *doyng-doyng-doyng!*

"Finally!" says Robby, who is not among the sleepers. Meaning, finally, it's three o'clock. "Kudjoocome! Kudjoocome!" the voice echoes throughout the apartment.

"Kudjoocome"—a mispronunciation of "Could you come?" and in Robby's family, a sacred ceremony not to be missed, an hour of pure happiness, caressed by the afternoon sun.

They emerge from every corner of the house and convene in the parents' bedroom, around the wide bed with its rumpled summer comforters. A ceremony of familial privacy. No guest shall dare enter this holy place. Once, Victor Hamdi-Ali tried to sneak into the room, and was immediately pushed out shamefully by Grandma and Robby.

Robby's father is already sitting on the bed, reclined against an abundance of pillows, leisurely and distractedly flipping through an Émile Zola novel. It's a 1925 edition, and the pages are already yellowing, their edges crumbling.

Robby's mother is in the room too, wearing a robe over her nightgown, her straight black hair running along her pure ivory face, tainted only by its rosy cheeks.

Robby puts away his coin collection, inherited from his brothers who migrated to Israel a year ago, and runs into the room, bouncing on the bed and wrapping his arms around his father's neck to get a kiss that smells of cologne and Player's Navy Cut cigarettes. Robby immediately spots the aforementioned surprise: a long envelope, no doubt a letter from his brothers. The letter, indeed, is from Israel, but the envelope and the stamps are from

France. Three weeks ago, maybe a month, his brothers wrote to their parents in Alexandria, but sent the letter to the town of Périgueux in France, to the house of Suzette Charnière. They met Suzette a year prior, during a training session run by the Jewish Agency on a farm in France. The training was meant to prepare the young men for agricultural life in Israel, but was mostly spent running around with local girls. Suzette fell head over heels for Robby's middle brother, and even after he left her all by her lonesome and went to Israel, she still hoped he would return and marry her. Whether out of practical calculations or pure altruism, she agreed to mediate between her beloved and his relatives, and never even asked Robby's brother to pay for the postage. At first, Robby's brother added to the Alexandrian letter a long letter for Suzette herself. Later on, the letters addressed to her grew shorter, and their passion dwindled, and finally the letters to the parents arrived on their own. Suzette swallowed the insult and continued to serve her role dutifully, as was fitting of a true Christian.

Robby yearns to rip the stamps off the envelope, but, seeing his father's stern expression, holds his horses. Order must be maintained in the Kudjoocome ritual.

Grandma joins the meeting, commenting on the hopelessly slow servants: "*Haraganos primos*, first-class bums."

Silence. Robby watches the daggers of sunlight invading between the shutters. In a moment, Salem will enter, pushing out the shutters to the expanses of air and light. The sun will burst inside with a lighthearted frivolity, and the ceremony will begin. This is all contingent on Robby's sister joining them on time.

"Where's Miss Anabella?" Father asks, using his nickname for Robby's sister.

"She's always late!" Robby tries to incite his father.

"It takes her forever to grace us with her presence, *esta cocona*!" Grandma adds her own fuel to the fire.

Steps approach. They all exhale, prepared to torment the tardy party with their righteous rebukes, and Grandma already begins spewing her share, but they are disappointed when it is only Salem the servant who enters the room. He carries a tray of small cups of Greek coffee and glasses of ice water with pearls of condensation. Finding his masters laughing, he joins the hoopla, not knowing what it is about, but trusting his heart that playing along will win him his masters' favors. He hands out coffee and water by way of a little dance, while Grandma tells him off, saying that his twirls will cause the coffee to lose its *kaimak*, that layer of brown foam, without which the beverage can barely be called coffee. He immediately puts on an expression of grave servitude, continuing his waiter's ballet in *moderato*.

Robby does not get coffee, of course, because Grandma says that kids who drink coffee *pishan preto*—piss black. (The mere thought of a black spray painting the toilet water puts Robby in a state of panic. He runs to the bathroom. Thank God, the color is normal.) Instead, he receives sickly sweet cocoa, sipping it with a pleasure whose very memory brings sweetness to his stomach years later.

The tray is empty. Salem opens the shutters wide and then stands around, smiling proudly, as if he himself had created the sun. They all look at him gratefully and dismissively, but Salem does not budge. Perhaps he'll hear a snippet of conversation, or maybe his master will inform him of a raise. All signs point to his expectations being met: Robby's father says, "Listen, Salem, starting next month —" but Grandma foresees the future and quickly orders Salem to go and call "*mamazel*'" to join them for "*kushkucome*"—a mispronunciation of a mispronunciation, meant to awaken laughter and push aside the matter of the raise. Salem shifts from foot to foot for a moment longer, perhaps his master will recall his initial intention, but his alert black eyes, bouncing around like those of a smart animal, slam against the wall of laughter. He has no choice but to go do as he is ordered. Maybe next time …

They wait.

Grandma is burning with curiosity, and pleads with Robby's father to begin reading the letter without waiting for his daughter. But of course he won't. The three thin pages of the letter make crispy rustlings in his hand, stimulating his appetite for words, but he restrains himself. When he placed *La Faute de l'Abbé Mouret* on the bed next to him, he also removed his glasses, so he wouldn't be tempted to take a peek at the letter. Now he sips from the thick coffee, a wondrous mixture of spicy and sweet. "We'll wait for Miss Anabella!"

"Ana-bella, Ana-bella, like a seesaw!" Robby grabs hold of his toes and rocks back and forth on the bed, Ana-bella, Ana-bella, Ana-bella, but he does not ignite sympathy or laughter, only reproaches, as he is about to spill someone's coffee on the bed.

"Is there any coffee left for me?" sounds the relaxed, indulgent voice of the aforementioned Miss Anabella. She is wearing a nightgown, her auburn hair is wild, her eyes are puffy. An enormous yawn swallows the word "me." Sleepwalking, she goes to the dresser and searches for the delicate china cup with the image of a marquis asking a marquise to dance. Only after taking a long sip and sighing deeply does she manage to open one eye and stare at her surroundings, her free hand grabbing the arm of her chair.

Grandma informs her that a letter has arrived from "the children." Miss Anabella sits up and says, "Really? When?"

"This afternoon. Your father brought it back from the office. They sent it straight to Ford." The fact of the letter, along with two more sips of coffee, completely erases the sleep from her eyes, and she is awake and smiling and rearing to go, even prepared to give Grandma a fight. Grandma wastes no time: "What does it say, you ask? How should we know? You think we've read it? Your father insisted that we wait for you, while you were lying around in bed like a *cataplasmo*." One would not imagine she would make do with such a benign comment, especially seeing how the indifference and laziness on the face of her opponent only feed her desire to fight, but at that moment the father puts on his glasses with equanimity and determination that announce the commencement of the reading.

Silence.

"'Dear family, we apologize for not having written in so long ...'"

"That's right!" Grandma confirms.

"'We were just very busy. We left the place where we lived until now ...'"

"That's the *koobooss*," Grandma interprets needlessly, since the boys have already hinted in a previous letter that they'd been living on a kibbutz.

"'To the place where Felix's family lives.'"

"To Tel Aviv," Grandma adds. This language of riddles is a necessity, since the Egyptian secret police occasionally opens letters addressed to Jewish families, and those must not contain any express details about Israel. That's why the authors of these letters make up primitive codes in order to provide important information. Some even agree with their relatives in advance that Italy means Israel, Genoa means Haifa, Milan is Tel Aviv and Rome is Jerusalem. There is a story about Raoul Picciotto, who went to Italy with the Israeli Basketball League to play basketball for two weeks and invited his old mother in Alexandria to visit him in Genoa. Virginie Picciotto, the widow, immediately understood that Genoa meant Haifa, and was overjoyed that her son finally remembered her and invited her to join him in Israel. She did wonder how her soft son managed to convince his wife, her daughter-in-law, that witch, to have his mother live with them, but she quickly erased any doubt or embarrassment from her mind, and two weeks later was on a ship bound for Israel. When the ship entered the Haifa port at the agreed upon time, her son was waiting for her at the port of Genoa.

"And the expression on the face of Elvire Picciotto, her daughter-in-law, who stayed in Israel, when she saw her mother-in-law at her doorstep, was a sight to behold!" Madame Marika always concludes the story, which very well may be merely a figment of her imagination.

"Money is worthless here!" Robby's two brothers announce unanimously in their letter. This is, of course, the time of austerity in Israel of the early 1950s. Even those who had funds could not buy any more than what was allocated to them in their food coupons. Naively, the two boys remained blind to the flourishing black market, where money buys everything, just like anywhere else in the world.

"'Here they eat money, because there's nothing else to eat!'"

"*Wy-di-mi-no!*" Grandma calls, prepared to lament, but her son-in-law stops her by raising his voice, and indeed the next sentence is more encouraging: "'But all in all, the atmosphere is cheerful and we're happy! Except that we miss you. Come join us!'"

"You see?" Robby's mother rebukes her mother. "No need to worry. They're young, they'll be all right."

"They say that people work in construction in Palestine. Yes, even educated boys. A grandson of mine, putting his hand inside the *cemento*? Wy-di-mi-no!"

"*Bass-ba'ah!* Enough, Grandma, knock it off!" This time Robby's father is forced to explicitly demand silence in Arabic. Grandma swallows her insult along with her tears and makes a face like a punished baby's.

Near the end of the letter, Father reads: "'Is it true

what people here are saying, that David Hamdi-Ali is going to marry Lilly Elhadeff?'"

All goes quiet. Even in Tel Aviv, where people buy meat for food points, David Hamdi-Ali's love life is a conversation. All eyes turn to Robby's sister, but she just shrugs. A blush spreads across her cheeks and contradicts her indifferent expression. It's true, she does not fancy Hamdi-Ali the son, but neither is she prepared to release him from her leash. And the idea that Lilly Elhadeff ... of all people ... who doesn't even have any tits ... no matter, justice will be done ...

While she ponders this new discovery, trying to draft up a revised action plan, Grandma's response already sings through the air: "I'm glad. I'm glad! You see, *bovica*, you fool. How long do you think he'll wait for you? By the time you move your *como-se-yama*, he'll be married to that *Madame Ouevo*, that egg-face."

Robby's sister blows out an indulgent exhale and announces that she's going to get dressed, because she is invited to a cruise at the Nautical Club.

"With David Hamdi-Ali?" Grandma asks, all atwitter. But "Miss Anabella" feels no urge to satisfy her grandmother's curiosity and turns to leave with a mysterious smile. Grandma nevertheless appeases the others: "It's with him, it's with him!"

"Why are you meddling?" Robby's father asks her reproachfully and shakes his head. His motto, "Never interfere"—in English—goes for his sons and even his daughter. One cannot expect, of course, that Grandma also adopt this sort of *inglese* habit. His eyes fall on *La Faute de l'Abbé Mouret*, rolling around between the folds of the blanket, like a raft lost among waves. His eyes reflect a yearning for faraway worlds he's never visited. How did the ambitions of the past sink into oblivion? How did the taste for adventure that pulsed through him in his youth become so dulled? Travels to foreign, mysterious lands, dabbling in writing... everything evaporated inside this lovely, loosening comfort. This Alexandria ... this laziness ... this Kudjoocome.

He looks at his youngest son, at Robby, and says nothing. Wordlessly, Robby wraps his arms around his father's neck and kisses the cologne on his cheek.

9. Another Baba au Rhum

"Well then, it's true!" Robby's sister sticks the fork in the spongy flesh of a plump baba au rhum cake with a white crest of whipped cream. Her large, light-brown eyes fix David with an accusatory gaze. He turns away from her. They've just returned from a cruise on a rented sailboat, and David proudly proved that he could control not only a horse's reins, but also the ropes of a vessel, all the while maintaining a smiling energy as Robby's sister sat in the stern, staring at him with the ridiculing smile of the Sphinx.

She always makes me feel like an idiot! David says to himself as they sit in the café of the Nautical Club. For a moment, a hint of hatred flits through his heart. If she only said yes, simply, with a delicate smile and lowered eyes, with gratitude, with modesty ...

"Well then, it's true," she repeats. She eats her baba au rhum lustily, as if to make him jealous. He cannot eat any, on account of his strict diet. Instead he sits there, watching the whipped cream disappear between her lips.

"You know that if you only say yes ... if you only give me a sign ..."

"Meaning, it's true, Lilly Elhadeff, huh? You've made a laughingstock out of me!" she says, pushing away her empty plate. The fork scrapes the china in protest.

"I'll make you a queen, if you only say yes. That's all I ask!"

"How can I say yes while Lilly Elhadeff is waiting with bridesmaids and bouquets?" she asks with a half-smile. Simultaneously, she wonders: Will this cheapskate offer me another baba au rhum?

"Just give me a sign and I'll tell Lilly Elhadeff to go to hell!"

"You don't tell a girl to go to hell, my dear gentleman," Robby's sister admonishes. "And I won't tell you what to do, David Hamdi-Ali!"

"I'm going crazy! Because of you I can't even focus during races. Yesterday I nearly flew off the horse …"

"Soon you'll blame me for all your failures, huh? What do you want from me? Go marry Lilly Elhadeff. Poor guy! I pity you, *mon chouchou*."

"You're suggesting that I marry her? You're pushing me into her arms?"

"Look, if you don't have anything better, even Lilly Elhadeff is something. Not the brightest, but she knows how to cook, which I don't. She isn't exactly Cleopatra, but her father has a big store in Heliopolis. My father is only a clerk at Ford. And if she isn't a dream girl for someone like you, at least …"

"At least she isn't capricious!" David finishes her sentence, his patience about to run out. "What do you want? What do you want? Tell me!"

"Thanks for asking, David. I want … I want … another baba au rhum. Will you get me one, please?"

10. I'll Make You a Queen

Sunday, the day the racing season commences, is to be David Hamdi-Ali's day to shine.

All day Saturday David was seen striking any and all athletic poses that a strong, agile body can show off. In shiny white shorts and a blinding undershirt that accentuated his muscular chest, he pranced around the house, hopping and leaping and inhaling and exhaling and massaging himself, his fair eyes turned inward in introspection, as if saying, "There could be no other."

He was so preoccupied, he hadn't even noticed Robby's sister as she ran to the balcony in a thin batiste dress and waved down to the Coptic lawyer, Maître Habib Ramzi, who waited downstairs in a black Citroën. David didn't seem to even notice her about to go out with his chubby competitor, his skin the shade of café-au-lait.

"I'll be right down," Robby's sister called to the lawyer, leaning against the railing. But when she returned to the hall she looked distractedly at the boy shaking his limbs every which way, the boy who could be hers if she only gave him a sign. Perhaps she recalled his declaration, made only a week before, at the casino in the San Stefano neighborhood: "I'll make you a queen. A queen!" That's what he repeated at the nautical club. She might have even thought at that moment, "Why not?" Perhaps she expected something to happen, for him to wave his hand, bat his lashes, show her she was more important than the Sunday race. But whether because this wasn't the case, or because he was distracted, or maybe even due to a vengeful cockiness, this small, tender, fluttering moment was missed. Another honk from the Citroën, a stroke of sunlight from the balcony, eliminating the dimness of the hall, and the moment was gone.

Robby's sister turned to the door, smiling to herself. Walking down the stairs, she might have been thinking, "What a lucky break, that was a close one. I almost got myself into trouble." With rollicking laughter, she walked out to the sidewalk. Maître Ramzi saw her mirth as a good sign and his face beamed. His features always reminded Robby of the Reclining Scribe, an ancient Egyptian sculpture of the pharaonic age.

From the balcony, Robby watched his white sister

being swallowed up inside the black car. For a moment he wondered how she could go out with such a fat, ugly specimen, and a Christian to boot! He looked at the sky and recalled the iron cross pointing from the church tower in the Camp *César* neighborhood, and remembered his fanatical declaration, which shocked his parents: "One day I'll climb to the top of that tower and break that cross!"

This didn't stop him from loving the two Coptic sisters Thérèse and Juliette Murad, who, along with their mother, Angélique, rented the large room facing the sea. Thérèse with her white skin and black hair, and Juliette with her blond braids: on both chests—one round and the other boyish and flat—hung small golden crosses that pierced Robby's flesh when the high school girls hugged him with motherly affection.

Suddenly he heard David's tenor voice rumble from the cavernous hall, "Get out of here! Get out!"

Robby ran to the hall and saw a white figure in the dark: David Hamdi-Ali in his workout clothes. Slowly, from the darkness, rose two rows of white teeth, as big as a horse's, a mane of mop-like blond hair and finally two watery eyes, groveling and rebelling at once, their lashes fluttering. Victor stood before his brother, as stiff as a martyr, only his protruding Adam's apple bobbing, working to block the humiliation of oncoming tears. He stood there in his loose, slightly soiled underwear, a dry pee stain (Robby could not know at the time that it might have been something else) forming a strange halo around his crotch. For a moment, Robby's heart was also filled with disdain toward the rebuked child. How different was this gangly, mean satyr from his virile, white Apollo of a brother. Without caring to find out the matter at hand, Robby immediately took the older brother's side. He wanted to stomp the vermin, but his father had taught him never to intervene in others' business, and especially not in familial feuds. Still, his presence seemed to encourage David, who stood up from his workout pose, walked over to his brother and muttered, "You'll get out of here, or I'll ..."

But Victor stood his ground, and Robby was already expecting the whack of the slap. His friend's pointless stand annoyed him, and he couldn't wait to see him defeated. That moment, Emilie walked in and called out in a soft, fearful voice, "Why do you want to hit him, David?"

Her fragile voice seemed to have popped his balloon of aggression. David put his hands on his head and said in a childlike voice that Robby had never heard coming from the lips of a man, "Mama, he's annoying me. He brings me bad luck. Mama, I'm going to lose the race tomorrow because of him! Mama ..." He ran to her, perhaps to bury his head in her bosom, but then thought better of it and went into his room. Emilie looked at her two sons for a moment and seemed to understand nothing. To her, life was so simple!

"Come have lunch," she told Victor and was immediately relieved. For Emilie, just like for Robby's grandmother, food was a cure-all. Her eyes lit up and she went to the kitchen.

Victor stayed in place, looking at Robby triumphantly. Without further ado, he pounced on him with fists pumping. The two boys rolled around on the rug for a while, and Robby could feel Victor's sharp bones pushing against his body. Suddenly he felt his friend's erect penis knocking persistently against his body. Chills of shame shook his entire being, and he tried to pull away from this embrace. His heart whispered to him that this was a new thing, entirely new. He'd never known such a feeling, not even when Thérèse and Juliette hugged him. Finally, he pulled out of Victor's grasp. The two of them stood before each other, silent and breathing heavily.

11. NEFERTITI

Sunday, the day of the beginning of racing season, would be a very busy day at the apartment on 24 Rue Delta. Apart from the race, which was scheduled for four in the afternoon, and from which children were banned, Robby planned a big party that evening. The program was full: Thérèse would play a piece on the antique German piano, maybe *La danse du feu*, as well as background music for the dance of Nefertiti, to be performed by no other than Robby himself. Endless debates were held in an attempt to re-create the sounds of ancient Egyptian music. Juliette would recite two fables by the beloved La Fontaine. Even Marcel, Robby's cousin, who could play Monti's *Csárdás* on the violin as fast as an express train, would do his part. And finally, Raphael, Robby's other cousin, would close the program with songs in Spanish, and would be the star of the evening, because, unlike the other performers, Raphael was a grownup, and performed regularly at the Auberge Bleue.

After the entertainment, the drinking would commence, arak or liquor for the grownups, Pepsi or Coke for the kids, in celebration of David's victory (no one even considered the possibility of a loss).

The morning was spent in preparation. Thérèse and Juliette hung up colorful garlands and Chinese lanterns. Robby and his mother joined forces to prepare his Nefertiti costume. Robby's grandmother and Emilie supervised the kitchen, where the servants were hard at work, preparing a range of Balkan refreshments, passed from Jewish mothers to their daughters for generations: the square *boyos* and the triangular *burekitas*, the donut shaped *biscochicos* and even *baklava*. The *kunafah*, that sweet, thin-as-a-wisp *kadaif* delicacy, would be bought from the vendor on the street corner.

Only Victor seemed to purposefully avoid participating, walking around the house with his underwear hanging over his sunken gut, looking at everybody with derision and not lifting a finger. He didn't hand the scissors to Thérèse who stood on the chair, hanging garlands from the curtain rods to the chandelier, and didn't help Robby tie Nefertiti's upside-down bucket crown around his head, and refused to even go downstairs to buy some string at Hamis's store for the decorations. Everyone was cross with him at first, but they quickly learned to ignore him.

The house was full of hustle and bustle and the radio played and the sun was shining. A festive feeling was in the air. Tino Rossi swept everyone up with his *Tarantelle Belle-belle*, and the two Coptic sisters laughed happily after whispering among themselves. Robby was in high spirits. Suddenly, Victor called him over and he followed. Victor signaled to him to keep quiet and pulled him into one of the back rooms of the apartment, where the ruckus from the hall sounded like a strange, distant hum. Victor chuckled and pointed at the heavy wine-colored velvet curtain. There was nothing in that old curtain to justify Victor's glee. Not a cigarette hole or a bug or a gecko. Victor nudged him toward the window and pushed the curtain slightly open. A thin blade of golden dust cleaved the darkness of the room in two, and Robby brought his eye closer to the crack. At first he saw nothing. The sun's reflection on the window across the way blinded him. It was the window of the Abarbanell apartment, where Louis Abarbanell, Robby's best friend, lived. His eyes gradually adjusted to the blinding beams of the scorching glass. Suddenly he could see clearly: by the window stood a woman of middle age, naked from the waist up. The woman lifted her left breast to examine some pink mark that had formed there. She then picked up a satchel and sprinkled some talcum powder on the aroused skin. Robby wished to escape. "That's ... That's Dora Abarbanell, Louis's mother ..." He was as hurt as if his own mother had been standing there, prey to Victor Hamdi-Ali's covetous eyes. But Victor's heavy, hot breath weighed down the back of his neck like a stifling burden, and his hard member knocked on the doors of his body, trying to push in. Cold sweat covered his face. The sight of the large breasts growing before his eyes like a pair of balloons, and the sensation of the persistent force, striving restlessly to invade him, enveloped him with breathless confusion. The two giant nipples twinkled at him lecherously from their pink halo. Suddenly he imagined Michel Abarbanell, Dora's ex-husband, whom she divorced years ago, when Louis was just a baby; a shrunken man, his gray face resembling that of the pharaoh mummies in the museum in Cairo, and his hair, also done-up in Golden Age Egyptian style, combed back carefully and treated with brilliantine. He always wore a pressed suit, and did not look like a divorced man who'd spent the past eight years without the care of a woman. When Robby saw the hidden treasures of the ex-wife's breasts, he pitied him, this Michel, who was so small and shriveled in comparison to the full, udder-like flesh that filled the window frame. The lump in his throat grew. Suddenly he was scared that Dora might raise her eyes and look at him accusingly. A false fear, of course, since he was standing in the darkness, protected by the heavy curtain. After what felt like an eternity he managed to free himself of Victor's grip and escape to the hall, where no one had even noticed his absence.

Grandma's friends started to arrive. Grandma demanded that the center of the hall be cleared for the card table.

"Robby, come show the ladies your Nefertiti costume!"

"But it's a surprise for tonight."

"Yes, but we won't be here tonight," said Madame Marika, and added with an offended air, "We weren't invited."

"You ... you're invited," Robby mumbled, not even trying to sound sincere.

"But there's an entrance fee," Grandma warned them. "This is no regular party. There are going to be live shows."

"A fee!" the ladies exclaimed. "How much? How much is it, Robby?"

"One piaster per person."

"With one piaster you can buy two portions of falafel in pita," Madame Marika protested loudly and immediately burst into a thousand shreds of laughter.

"Or take the tram to Place Muhammad-Ali," Madame Geena added, laughing as well.

"No, that's too rich for my taste. If I spend this piaster, Isidore, my husband, will kill me!" Alice called, and now the women who hadn't been laughing joined in on the merriment; they despised Isidore for his objecting to Alice's card playing. A man like Isidore was a risk for all of them, since other husbands might decide to follow suit and question the women over their addiction to the seductions of the joker. Alice herself was glad to have elicited her friends' sympathies, and saw their laughter as support in her brave battle against the tyrant.

Robby stood before them and thought, They're speaking to me like I'm a baby. This kind of fake seriousness is used with babies. They don't even see how ridiculous they are. They also have a pair of hanging breasts, just like Dora Abarbanell's, so what have they got to be so happy about?

He tried to evade them, but they asked again that he wear his costume for them, and his mother also urged him, wanting to show off her work. And so Robby gave in.

Embarrassed and ashamed, but also excited to have all eyes on him, Robby found his way between the folds of the long dress, which grew wide around the ankles. A small beach bucket was atop his head, its narrow base acting as the famous conical crown of the stunning Egyptian queen. For scepters he had his father's fly swatter, nicknamed "Can't Miss," as well as—no lie—David Hamdi-Ali's whip, which he used to spur his horse, Esperance.

"Like a girl … just like a girl!" the women cheered. Robby blushed, but never took his eyes off them, and even tried to afford himself a regal air of condescension. All of them, all of them, other than the venerable Madame Livia, all of them fat with big butts, too big for the narrow seats to accommodate, *culos*, as his grandmother says when she's cross with them. He was happy to see them in their wretchedness, laughing and purring and shaking their bellies. Only the beautiful, proud Madame Livia earned his respect and reverence. "Like a girl, like a girl."

In a shaded corner, Robby noticed the twisting silhouette of the gloating Victor, making lewd gestures with his fingers, the kind he'd only ever seen the Arabs make.

"When he was born," Grandma said, "did I ever tell you this story? When he was born, little Robby, oh, how his sister cried …"

"You don't say!" Madame Marika exclaimed in false wonder. She'd heard the story before, but wanted to please Grandma.

"Yes. Because she wanted a sister. When she heard she had a little brother instead, *no demandes*! Don't ask!" Grandma mimicked her granddaughter's wails, to the pleasure of the *coconas*: "Send him back! Exchange him at the store!"

"What?" Madame Marika called. "Eleven years old and she still didn't know kids didn't come from the store?"

Grandma poked her elbow in Madame Marika's rib cage, to remind her that the child was listening. With amazing speed, Marika changed the planned ending of her sentence and said, "Didn't she know the stork brings them?"

Victor couldn't help himself anymore, and let out an

ugly moan, which could be easily confused with something else, and then burst into teasing laughter and escaped. The women were shocked and upset.

"I didn't know until I turned nineteen," Grandma said and started laughing again. "We were such fools back then!" All the women laughed again. Robby used the opportunity to get away as well, almost falling flat on his face when his legs got caught in the dress. The bucket on his head slid down to his nose and bruised it a bit. The pain was bearable, but the insult burned, and he cried in his mother's lap and wished a plague on the houses of all the members of the card club.

12. A Very Nice Game

Slowly, the sounds of laughter and gaiety died down, and around three o'clock a strange silence fell upon the house. Everyone was at the races, and Robby stayed home alone with Victor. The racetracks were closed to children. The two of them stood on the balcony and watched silently as the festive crowds moved along the sidewalk of Rue Delta toward the Sporting Club racetracks, beyond the tram tracks. The women in white, fluttering summer dresses, wide-brimmed hats and small sun umbrellas. The men in flashy, enviable white faux-silk or dazzling sharkskin suits. A carefree group, yearning for pleasure on this hot, sunny, humid summer's day. A light, salty, tickling wind rose from the sea, waving the tulle ends of hats, and mischievously raising a dress up over someone's knees, to Victor's snorts of satisfaction. Robby placed his cheek against his folded arms upon the cool railing and dozed off, his half-closed eyes watching a white fog of woolly clouds, moving in soporific waves. When he awoke, the sidewalk was empty and the clouds were gone, as if a sorcerer had made them disappear with a flick of his magic wand. Suddenly, he heard Victor's steady snorts, his heavy breathing. Only then did he feel a strange percolation sending vibrations through his body. His underwear was like a tent, and Victor's hard penis rubbed against him, back and forth. Though he knew very well that this was crude behavior, he did nothing to stop his friend, and even pretended to still be asleep and gave in to the pleasure, feeling a charge of power flowing and releasing from the tip of his penis. He pushed his body up against the wall of the railing, shoving his burning gut at the rough coolness. A strong, pleasant pain spread through him.

Suddenly he heard Victor whispering, "Now it's your turn." At first he didn't understand, but then he felt Victor slowly separating from his body and taking his hand and leading him into the house. For a while they walked carefully through the dark hall, as if they'd found themselves in a cave. The first thing Robby saw clearly was the pink hook between Victor's legs, flapping around like a small, quick animal, like some sort of reddish, restless rat. In his hurry, Victor managed to grab a large pillow, and now dropped it to the ground, lay on top of it and spread open his behind to expand his rectum. The sight of the brown hole made Robby feel nauseous, but before he could even tell what was going on, he was ripping into his friend's body. A heavy, sour smell of sweat. The stench almost choked him, but also awoke a wondrous animal lust within him.

"And that's nothing," Victor chirped, clicking his tongue. "Just imagine what it's like to do this to a girl!"

"To a girl? Just like this? In the ass?"

"No," Victor whispered, "in the front." He stretched out his neck and laughed his nervous laugh.

"In, in her front?" Robby didn't understand. His imagination, shaped by the agreed-upon, petit bourgeois norms of Alex, was incapable of picturing such fantastical things.

"Yes, where she pees from."

"But ... but it's so small."

"What's so small?"

"The hole."

"How do you know? Have you seen one?"

"No, I haven't."

"I have." Victor's blue eyes shot flames. "Our servant in Cairo has a little girl ..."

Robby was appalled. With the remains of his strength, he asked, "And you ... you ... did you do it?"

"No, her whore of a mother caught us just when I was about to stick it to her, because that little stupid girl was crying. Damn!"

"Stick it to girls?" Robby mumbled. The thought didn't make him feel any passion, only disgust. He was getting accustomed to the idea that boys could enjoy this, and though their parents would probably be angry if they caught them, the pleasure was worth the risk. But with girls ... he was embarrassed by the mere idea of a girl seeing him naked.

"You idiot, what are you so surprised about? That's how you were born."

"Me?"

"Not *just* you, *also* you. Your parents ..."

"No! It can't be." Robby didn't want to hear one more thing. He'd believed Victor so far, but the idea of his parents, his mother and father, naked in bed, and his father ... and his mother ... Robby was appalled and wanted to hear nothing more. He stopped listening and only heard a muffled version of the rest of the lesson on reproduction: "And the sperm ... the semen ... like milk ... but not like the milk you drink, more like Nestle condensed milk ... and there ... in the woman's hole ... it gets bigger, and there's a baby inside."

"And I thought that ... that the wine the parents drink when they get married ..."

Victor's laughter was wild. He turned over and jerked around on the rug, naked. Finally he lay still, helpless and satisfied.

13. HE SEES YOU!

The doorbell rang. Have they all returned from the race already? For a moment the children panicked. Victor quickly pulled on his pants and scampered around, awkward and confused, all his bravery and gusto evaporating. Suddenly he grabbed Robby's arm and stuttered, "You won't tell anybody, will you?"

"Of course not," Robby said, a wave of guilt sending a deep blush to his cheeks.

"Because if you do," Victor tried to transfer his own fear into Robby, "they'll beat you up. They'll kill you."

"No one will touch me," Robby said proudly. "My father never lays a hand on me. But your father and big brother will beat you to death!" He found satisfaction and a sense of supremacy in the thought. It was his small revenge for all those childhood myths violently shattered by Victor's hot breath. He was still shaken by the vision of his father and mother, naked in bed, in coitus, doing just as he and Victor had done. He ran to open the door, ready to confess everything he'd done, ready to bear the punishment, whatever it may be.

"What are you doing here?"

At the door was Claude Cohen, chubby and bespectacled, grinning broadly.

"What are you doing here?" Robby repeated.

"What am I doing here? You invited me. Me and Isaac and Maxie Ephraim."

"Isaac and Maxie?"

"You said we'd play with marbles. In your hall, on the rug."

"Here, in the hall, on the rug?"

Victor came out and glanced at the guest with a curious smile. Claude was wearing a white suit with a red tie. His shorn hair was covered with a small, red newsboy cap with the initials "C.C." embroidered in gold. A pampered little boy. Victor's bouncy eyes could already see the suit folded carefully on the chair, and Claude lying on the rug, his round, white behind served up as if on a platter. Victor trembled with expectation and said in a hoarse voice, "Do you want ... want to play with us, Claude?"

"Yes," said Claude. "What are you playing?"

"A very nice game," said Victor. "Right, Robby?"

"Ye...es," Robby stuttered.

"You want us to show you how to play so you can join us?"

"Is it a new game?" Claude asked naively, his smiling eyes shifting from one boy to the next.

"A new game," Victor laughed. "Robby wants to show you."

"No," Robby called out with alarm.

"Why not?" asked Victor.

"Why not," asked Claude, "is it dangerous?"

Robby could imagine himself playing all these forbidden, even dirty games, as they'd been categorized in his puritanical mind, with Victor. He could file away and push aside all these acts in a secret drawer, never to be discussed. But he could never imagine this good little boy—his parents were an elderly couple blessed in their old age with little Claude and they treated him with kid gloves—agreeing to bare his dainty behind and receive Victor's iron rod. He would probably escape, disgusted, and that would be the end of their friendship. Robby knew that Victor was trying to push him away from his other friends, jealous and wanting full control of him. Claude mustn't know that he'd been seduced by Victor, mustn't even suspect it. But while he busied himself with these thoughts, Victor was already standing before them, naked as the day he was born, wagging his reddish penis.

Claude was confused. "What's going on? Does he need to pee?"

Victor twisted on the rug again in a wild dance of laughter. Finally he said, "I want ... I want to show you the game we've been playing."

"What, you play this game naked?" Claude asked incredulously. His English nanny, Miss Pleasance, would probably advise against such games, but ... to hell with his nanny! Claude looked at Robby expectantly, hoping for confirmation. Robby shrugged. Whatever happens, happens! He sat down on the armchair and watched Victor, who didn't hesitate and whispered something in Claude's ear. Claude blushed, and immediately smiled. The more the devil whispered in his ear, the more his smile grew. It seemed that this delicate mama's boy was not disgusted by Victor's indecent offers in the least.

"Each of us will lie down in turn, and the others will stick it to him," Victor set the rules of the game. To prevent any potential objections, he volunteered to lie down first, and raised his thin, pointy, dirty behind. Claude quickly removed his clothes, not even taking time to arrange them carefully, as was his habit. He put all his weight on Victor and tried to push his tiny member into him, giggling with pleasure. He breathed hard, going up and down, and never stopped making sounds of liberated joy, a kind that Robby had never heard him make before, not even when they played with marbles.

"Enough!" Victor said. "Now it's Robby's turn."

"Already?" Claude grumbled, but he respected authority. Victor had taken on the role of Miss Pleasance, and he had to be obeyed. He stood up with a heavy breath, his penis, blushed with friction, hiding beneath his small white paunch, resembling the whitewashed dome of a mosque.

"Come on, Robby," said Victor.

Claude urged him on. "Don't you want to? You should, it's good."

"I know it's good, I knew it before you!" Robby announced. This little spoiled brat was going to tell *him* it was good? As if he wasn't already the more experienced one. He quickly undressed and pounced at Victor, who sounded a loud "Ayyy," Robby's weight almost breaking his bones, but then immediately closed his eyes and gave himself into that vibrating, caressing pleasure. What a difference between Robby's light agility and Claude's bear-like clumsiness. But it would all be worth it once it was his turn to ride Claude. A plump, soft behind held pleasures that surpassed even his wildest imagination.

"Now it's Claude's turn to lie down," Victor announced, barely stopping himself from jumping for joy. Claude obeyed at once, lying down on the rug and trying to mimic Victor's posture. It was hard for him to disguise the discomfort of lying on his stomach atop the coarse rug. His penis was pricked by the hard bristles, but he didn't say a word. Victor sensed his discomfort and suggested moving to the back room at the end of the hall, where there was a soft sofa. Robby objected vehemently. Victor argued that in the back room they'd be better protected from unpleasant surprises, because if anyone suddenly entered the room, they would have to cross the entire hallway, giving the kids time to get dressed and pretend to have been doing something else. "Besides," Victor added with an ingratiating smile, "this rug is too rough for Clau-Clau's fine skin."

Claude nodded happily, not protesting the nickname. Robby remembered that he himself tried to call him that once, and Claude got mad and forbade him from ever using the name again.

Robby stood his ground and refused to reveal the reason behind his objections: on the wall of the back room was a picture of a man in his thirties, dressed in fashion predating the Second World War, his hair slicked back carefully, his face grave, almost gloomy, unsmiling, his eyes penetrating and all-seeing, until you couldn't help but look away from his accusatory gaze. Accusatory? What did I do to deserve this look? Could he have ... no! He couldn't have known ... that picture was taken before I was born. Then why is he looking at me that way?

It was a photograph of his father.

Once, when he committed some prank in that room, one of his brothers came up to him and said, "Stop, *he* can see you!" Robby stopped immediately, and then his brother mocked him for it. Nevertheless, Robby couldn't imagine him and his friends humping one another in front of his father's stern, open stare. Of course he wouldn't tell them his reasoning, knowing they would mock him the way his brother had, and try to persuade him.

Seeing that this was a lost cause, Victor suggested going to his own parents' bedroom, emphasizing the proposition with a gallant gesture, to signal how much more generous than Robby he was. Claude ran ahead with excitement toward those soft pillows, and Robby could hear the springs of the mattress protesting as he landed.

When the brothers, Isaac and Maxie Ephraim, showed up, the three boys didn't even bother to get dressed and pretend to play marbles. The two new arrivals undressed with haste and joined in the fun, as though this had always been their favorite game.

14. Marcelino

After the kids left for their homes, Robby and Victor stood on the balcony and watched the red sun, reclining, heavy and dreamy, among soft pillowy clouds. A light breeze rose from the sea, caressing their flushed cheeks. They were united by their new secret, and Robby felt a kind of affection toward Victor. It was a nice game. A boys' game. The grownups were enjoying the race that was closed to children, but the children had their own little secret, they had a place where no grownups were allowed.

"I hope he loses," Robby heard Victor whisper.

"Who?"

"I hope he falls off his horse." Victor's voice trembled. "Just once. Have him break an arm or a leg. Not die, but have *something* happen to him." Then he kneeled, put his hands together and mumbled, "Dear Lord, please let something happen to him." This devil, kneeling like a Christian, saying a prayer to the God of Jews. "If you do this for me, I promise I ..."

But Robby didn't hear Victor's vow. He remembered Marcelino, a pale Italian boy who lived around the corner, right over Hamis's store. Marcelino had been sickly since birth. When Alexandria was plagued with cholera, he was at death's door. The doctors gave up and told his parents that only a miracle could save him. His mother took this literally and went to the church in the Ibrahamiya neighborhood, confessed her sins and prayed to Saint Anthony, vowing that if he spared her boy she'd devote his life to the church and change his name to Sant'Antonio. God made His choice, and perhaps the saint lent a hand too, and Marcelino healed. With Neapolitan vigor, his mother prepared to keep her promise. A deal is a deal. Since then, on Rue Delta, one might come across a skinny little boy wearing a heavy brown monk's cassock, the rope tied around his waist dangling lower than his ankles, gaily sweeping the sidewalk like a child dressed for carnival. Sant'Antonio!

Dusk already clutched the corners of buildings and began slowly hovering down and piling on the street. Suddenly, as if born from darkness itself, the lamp lighter appeared at the end of the alley on his bicycle, holding a long magic wand, at its tip a single small and stubborn flame which he used to light the gas lamps along the sidewalk. He didn't even get off his bike, but instead pedaled his way from lamp to lamp, naively believing that at the same time God was riding his heavenly bike in much the same fashion, lighting the stars in the sky. And indeed, the stars appeared one by one, their light yellow. The entire street was now dipped in a magical aura. It was the aura of Sant'Antonio, who would never again play marbles or hide-and-seek, his life now dedicated to prayer and study.

This untroubled street, which not an hour ago was bathed in sunlight, its head dipped in water, was now gripped by chills, and it hurried to wrap itself in a navy-blue sailor's coat with silver buttons. There, in the heart of the bluish silence of twilight, was a loud, bright spot of light. A group of people wearing white, a cheerful ruckus coming from the center of their circle. The spot of light disappeared into the fabric of dark blue velvet, and then lit up again under another streetlamp. Only the buzzing did not fade away, but rather grew stronger, morphing into roaring laughter, the laughter of joviality.

Victor looked at the light and knew. His prayers had not been answered.

David Hamdi-Ali had scored a sweeping victory over his racing opponent.

15. LEILA

From twenty years away, beyond lands, seas, oceans, exiles … as an archeologist wandering in the darkness of oblivion, carrying the flashlight of memory that lights small corners here and there: an ancient mural dolled up in red, yellow and gold; a fresco that had once known the blessing of sunlight; the diagonal rays of Aten, god of the sun, ending in tiny hands, giving the grace of sun to the

head of the pharaoh and the head of his adored Queen
Nefertiti.

Robby dances his Nefertiti dance. Only Aten himself
knows how this bashful boy found the courage to impro-
vise an ancient Egyptian dance. Thérèse, at the piano,
messes up *Samson and Delilah* as best she can, and only
Marcel the musician wrinkles his face at a tuneless note
that no one but him notices. Victor's disdainful eyes do
not break the ceremonial serenity of Robby's angular
motions. Only one small worry trembles in his heart, but
he does not show it: the overturned bucket, the fact that it
might once more fall on his nose, which is protected with
a pink bandage. But the bucket cooperates and stays put.

The dance went off without a hitch. Well, almost
without a hitch: in the middle of the show, while Robby
was certain that his audience was mesmerized, old Aunt
Tovula sighed and said, "*Pisharé!*" meaning, "time to pee,"
and even stood up to carry out her plans. This innocent
comment raised thunderous laughter that blurred the
impression made by the show. Seeing what she had done,
she sat back down with a teasing grudge. "*Qué hay? Ma qué
ténéche?*" she asked with protest. "What's wrong? What's
wrong with you?" Then her face softened and she turned
to Robby's mother for some affection: "*Qué diché?* What
did I say?" Several voices joined together to hush the old
lady and Robby bit his lips, but knew that the show had
to go on, and decided to ignore the incident. Slowly, the
tumult died down and the dance continued. Once it was
over, laughter broke out again at the sight of the poor old
aunt running urgently toward the bathroom. Now even
Robby allowed himself a small smile. Aunt Tovula was his
favorite, and he couldn't stay mad at her.

Somebody started to clap and the rest followed. Thus,
the honor of the dance was restored. Robby's face grew
serious again immediately. A light bow, the lightest, the
Queen of Egypt wouldn't bow very deeply, let alone with

this bucket atop her head, which might fall to the ground in a metallic clatter.

Thérèse used this opportunity to give Robby a suffocating, pre-maternal hug, until his head was pressed between the evil hardness of the bucket and the generous softness of her ripening breasts. Now that he'd tasted the fruit of the Tree of Knowledge, fed to him by Victor, he could no longer lean his head against this feminine tenderness without blushing and pulling away a little. The grownups laughed. Juliette wanted to hug him as well, but he wasn't there anymore. In a flash, he was in the back room, at the end of the hall, explaining that he had to change. He didn't turn on the light. It felt urgent to get out of these ridiculous women's clothes. Had he actually been good, or were they just making fun of him? He was mad at himself for not being able to let go of these maddening thoughts. Why can't he do anything simply and fully without pointless pondering? He stood in his underwear, looking out the window. The moonlight painted his body silver, and cool, damp air touched him in a light, pleasurable caress. The window across the street was dark—Dora and Louis Abarbanell were among the audience at his performance. He loved small, delicate, fragile Louis, torn between his love for his big, sad mother, and his yearning for his father, small and fragile like him. Every Sunday morning his father picked him up for a walk on the boardwalk, where he treated him to black, sticky licorice. Louis hated licorice, but never dared tell his father, so as not to hurt him. Once, Robby asked to join them on their walk, but Louis forbade it with burning zealotry. A child like Robby, growing up in a harmonious household, could never understand such a strong response.

He loved little Louis, and almost refused to skip a grade because of him. When they both started at the Alexandria Jewish School, the *Lycée de l'Union Juive*, (an exceptional institution with no religious affiliation and with classes taught mainly in French, with a skimpy hand-ful of Hebrew and Arabic and a bit more English), they were both immediately enrolled in second grade. They shared a desk and were happy. On the very first day, the teacher asked for a volunteer to come and draw anything they wanted on the blackboard. Robby went to the head of the class and drew a curvy De Soto, the newest model. The teacher was amazed. Children who can draw like that belong in third grade. During French dictation Robby had only four spelling mistakes—once he forgot an *s* at the end of a plural form, and another time he forgot to double a consonant—nothing major. Kids who can do dictation with only four mistakes belong in third grade. He already knew multiplication and division, though in a slightly different method than that taught by Madame Aguion.

"Who taught you all of this?" asked Mlle. Sasson, his homeroom teacher.

"My sister," Robby said proudly.

"You don't belong in second grade," she announced. "You belong in third grade!"

"And what about Louis?"

"Louis is little!" she determined.

"But …"

"You're moving to third grade. You're going to be an architect!" she prophesied.

"I don't want to skip a grade," he said gravely.

Mlle. Sasson's large eyes grew wider. Her thin, trans-lucent skin stretched over the bones of her skull. For a moment she didn't know what to say. Could it be? Why would a boy want to stay in a lower class when given the opportunity to move ahead?

"I want to be with Louis!" His stubborn eyes focused on the De Soto's round contours. He wished he could wipe that perfection away with a wave of a hand.

"Fine, sit down."

But the teacher didn't give up. She spoke with Madame Aguion, the principal, who spoke with Robby's parents. His parents convinced him to move to third grade, and he did. At the end of the year he was second in his class and won the *Tableau d'honneur*, a sign of appreciation for his achievements. Second, not first. Why not first? Two opponents fought him for the desired title: little Lilianne, with her fox-face and dimples, and Fifi, with the dreamy eyes and the deep, throaty voice. Lilianne came in third, and Fifi first. Robby thought: if I even know what love is, I think I love Fifi. She always had the right answers. She wasn't brilliant, but she was calculating and calm, making his heart twirl with her quiet, confident voice. Victor asked him that afternoon if he didn't want to screw Fifi, and Robby hated him for this intrusion upon his lofty emotions.

The sounds of Monti's *Csárdás*, played on the violin by Marcel, reached Robby's mind through a fog. He liked watching his cousin play: the closed eyes, the chin leaning against the instrument, the relaxed concentration, all in contrast with the quickness of the playing hand, a breathtaking striving toward perfection. A great future had been foretold for Marcel. Next to him was his younger brother, Roger. Roger was retarded. No one foretold anything for him. Children made fun of him, grownups nodded at him politely, and a wily tumor kept growing inside his brain, pushing everything off toward the walls of his skull. His face was covered in fresh, ugly bruises from the falls he had whenever he lost his balance. He died that very summer. Robby didn't go to the funeral. They tried to shield children from such harsh experiences. Roger's mother hardly shed a tear for him. His old nanny, who took devoted care of him through all his years of illness, cried her heart out.

Happily, thanks to Marcel's playing, Robby's entrance did not receive any attention. He was a star tired of the limelight, craving anonymity. He sat down next to his mother and leaned his head against her arm.

David Hamdi-Ali sat in the middle of the hall, very close to Robby's sister, and the two of them were in the midst of a giggly conversation, ignoring all the hints and gestures and even bitter words that let them know that their brash chatting was interrupting the recital.

Sunken between the sofa cushions, Robby's sister's warm breath tickling his face, David was the happiest man alive. His fast, agile horse, Esperance, had beat Ahmed Al-Tal'ooni's horse. He was proud. He finally broke the prestige of "unbeatable" Al-Tal'ooni, the Muslim jockey, the star who had come all the way from the wandering tribes of the Libyan Desert to the refined racetracks of Alexandria, and who instantly became the pet of the city's European women. Ahmed was black, skinny and shrunken as a carob that had dried in the sun. Among his proud, masculine tribe he was considered to be an unfortunate genetic mistake. His father barely acknowledged him, and all agreed that the rough desert, which had its own wise natural selection, would find the only solution for this strange creature. He was neglected and forgotten, exempt from any and all duties, and could give himself completely to his one passion: riding horses through the desert. Legend has it that one day the head of the Bedouin tribe threw a *hafla*, a feast, in honor of the British consul, who occasionally liked to put on a Lawrence of Arabia gown and visit tents and sit on the ground and eat with his hands. As part of the feast, the sheikh arranged a *Fantaziya*—an equestrian extravaganza starring the entire *shabab*, the gang of young, beautiful, strong tribe members. In the middle of the show, the mysterious black knight emerged from the heart of the desert, shocking everyone with riding skills never seen before from Mecca to Benghazi. The Muslims swore that this horseman was born of the desert, while the British consul mumbled, "Sir Ivanhoe, I presume?" raising polite laughter among the European posse. When the black knight unveiled his face, the amazement reached its crescendo. The consul's wife immediately decided to adopt the boy, turning him into the playboy of Alexandria's high and bored society. His highness did not think much of the idea, but since he was twice as old as his wife, he dared not stand in the way of her follies. The sheikh, the boy's father, saw it as his duty to decrease Ahmed's perceived value and revealed each one of his shortcomings, even going so far as offering her the pick of his fifty sons, all large and burly, a sight for sore eyes. But the lady insisted. The sheikh could not understand how such a beautiful woman could choose the ugliest, most crooked of them all, but since he didn't want to insult his guests, he agreed to give them the boy. The legend does not explicate the nature of the relationship between the lovely consul's wife and her insect-like adoptee, but reality shows us that the lady turned the wild beast into a star of the racetrack. His name was heard beyond the borders of Egypt, exciting the imaginations of quite a few European women.

David Hamdi-Ali was proud of having beaten a legend.

But that wasn't on his mind at that moment. Tonight she's mine, he thought. She's finally mine. Perhaps she'll even let me touch her breasts. Not by coincidence, a fake accident, but for real, and these hands will fondle them. Robby's sister wondered why he kept kneading his handkerchief. Damn! Those breasts, so close, yet so far. Will she let me kiss them? Maybe she'll let me touch them but not kiss them, or maybe she'll let me kiss them but not t... No, logic determines that she'll let me touch them but not kiss them, or maybe not even touch. Damn! Those breasts, so close, yet so far ...

Dried fruits, almonds and nuts were served. The *kadaif* and the *boyos* had already been brought out. Marzipan too, called *massapán* in Spanish, and called by Robby's grandmother *pita d'almendra*, almond pastry.

Robby's cousin Raphael, Aunt Tovula's son, whose

nickname for Robby was *Petit Tigre*, sang a song he improvised about Esperance, David's hope. Robby was immensely impressed. A more mature mind might not have been so taken with the song, but Raphael's voice was a clear tenor, and the applause was loud and enthusiastic. Grandma immediately asked him to sing the two songs that made him the toast of the Auberge Bleue: *Triana* and *Antonio Heredia Gitano*. He gladly obliged, and as he sang, Grandma couldn't help but accompany him and ruin the performance. "*Triana, mi Triana*," she called excitedly, her green eyes glowing. Occasionally she sang the lyrics before the music, as if announcing their approach, and other times she repeated lines, confirming them: "*ya viene'l dia, ya viene'l mare*, here comes the day, here come the waves!"

"*Yassoo!*" the guests cheered in Greek.

Por tu culpa culpita yo tengo
negro negrito, mi corason!
Your accusations make me feel guilty,
and evil thoughts fill my heart!

"*Es verdad!*" she finally said. It's true! No one knew for sure what she meant, what was so true.

Raphael asked Robby's grandmother to sing a song for him, and she refused, claiming to have a sore throat. The others began pleading. Finally she agreed to sing one dedicated to Raphaelico himself. When she began, no one could see the connection between this song, half Spanish and half Turkish, and Raphael. But when she reached the final lines, they all burst out laughing:

Antes eran maronchinos,
agora punios al garon;
No te paresca qu'es lo de antes,
agora te commando yo!

Even Blanche, Raphael's fiancée, laughed when he translated the song for her: I gave you cookies first, then fists straight to the neck. Don't think it's like before, now I'm in command. They were about to be married in the fall and move to Israel immediately after. Robby's grandma wasn't impressed with the pretty, smiling face of "*esta cocona*, Blanche," who came from Corfu. Grandma always said, "*Corfioto—loco!*" meaning, "Corfu natives—crazy!" claiming they should not be trusted. Years later, one scorching hot Israeli day in the desert town of Beer Sheba, when Raphael finally received signed divorce papers from Blanche, who made his life miserable, he sighed and admitted that his old aunt had been right, at least in his case.

David and Robby's sister used the first opportunity to abscond. The two mothers smiled. Robby's grandmother made an appropriate remark, and all agreed they were a fine-looking couple.

Suddenly, David's father spoke: "Today ... today a dream came true ... my dream." Then he closed his eyes and said no more. They all looked at him. He'd been so silent all day. Nobody expected to hear such a personal, dramatic statement from the quiet, fez-wearing man. Just like Victor, there was a kind of gloomy estrangement in Joseph Hamdi-Ali. You would never expect those pursed lips to let out such banal words, words that could have been spoken by any of the other guests.

The silence and the questioning looks did not confuse him in the least. He adjusted his fez and added, "It reminds me of my youth, when I myself was a jockey."

"You were a jockey, Mr. Hamdi-Ali?" someone tried to make friendly conversation.

But Joseph did not answer, only chuckled to himself, deep in his own world.

Emilie took it upon herself to explain. "You should have seen him. It was as if he were born on horseback!"

A hidden tremor rushed through her body. Light, hesitant lust swirled through her belly, sending waves to her breasts. She was grateful to Joseph for providing her with a beautiful life, and was proud to have given birth to such a handsome, wonderful boy as David.

"I used to have an Arabian mare, thin and noble. Leila was her name, because she was black *zay el-leil*, like the night. Her coat was smooth and shiny, you could pet her for hours, with her sounding little snorts of pleasure. One day, during a race, in a faraway country, she jumped over a hurdle and sprained her ankle as she landed. Leila knew one rule: you don't stop before the finish line. So she kept on galloping, turning the sprain into a fracture. She strode on three legs, the fourth one hanging limp in the air, and she made it fifty yards to the finish line before falling to the ground, writhing in pain. The vet tried to put a cast on her, but she refused any infringement on her freedom, and she kept jumping and twisting and moaning with pain. Poor Leila! Horses are not like men. They don't know that the cast or the bandage are meant to help, and they cannot make do with only three legs, because they need four to carry their weight. Especially a proud mare like Leila. She wasn't one to walk around helpless, and she wouldn't stop acting out, crying and hurting herself. There was no way to control her, and without the cast she had no chance to survive. My heart broke. I was the one who pulled the trigger …"

Tears choked him. In his mind's eye he saw Leila galloping in the dream tracks of his boyhood, all nobility and grace. He looked around him with cloudy eyes. He had no idea what the others thought of his story, nor did he care. His gaze was introverted. Suddenly he yearned to sit on the ground with his legs crossed and smoke a hookah and roll prayer beads between his fingers. Just like that, simply, endlessly, for a hundred years, two hundred, for eternity. Maybe that is heaven? A hookah and beads, into eternity?

He stood up, excused himself and went to his room, old and bent over, the fringe of his fez dancing happily against a miserable wrinkled face.

Everyone sat silent and gaping. No one had even noticed old Hamdi-Ali until then. It had seemed as if the Hamdi-Ali family story flowed along calmly on the surface, never penetrating the dark caves behind the quiet old man's eyes. And then, all of a sudden, a monologue. The man spoke, said his part and vanished into the shadows.

Robby looked at Victor and saw that he was close to tears. His pouting lips were trembling, and his appearance was somewhere between touching and pathetic. Robby wanted to make a gesture of sympathy. Victor saw this and twisted his face in ridicule, winked toward his father, chuckled and twisted his finger against his temple, as if saying, "My father's cuckoo!" Robby kept looking, and Victor could take no more and ran to his room. Robby didn't laugh at him.

The old clock chimed twelve.

A sigh of relief. The clock had broken the discomfort, giving someone reason to say, "What? It's midnight already? So late!"

That night, Robby dreamed of Leila, but couldn't remember his dream in the morning.

16. The Turk is All Man

Never rest on your laurels.

Never get blinded by fame.

Think about Ahmed's revenge race.

And most important—maintain a strict diet!

Mount your mare next Sunday without the overconfidence of the gullible rabbit racing against the wise turtle.

Nevertheless, do not forget that your victory last Sunday was a promise of future victories.

A promise for *you* to keep.

And one more thing—don't fall in love with your mare.

Remember what happened to your father, when he became attached to Leila with chains of love. Her tragic death killed my career. I became a trainer, but a trainer is but a pale shadow of the jockey, his pleasure and excitement merely shadows of the pleasure and excitement enjoyed by the jockey. The trouble is, other horses are merely the shadow of Leila. I could never get used to other horses. Don't fall in love with your mare, my son! Horses are more loyal than women, but they don't live as long.

David nodded and nodded, and his silent father sipped his Turkish coffee and talked and talked. They were alone on the balcony, in the light breeze. Joseph was not one for conversation. He was shy and uncomfortable around people. The scents of dainty women's perfumes and of the tobacco of cleanly-shaven men filled his heart with yearning for the smell of horses in their stable. He loved the noble silence of the horse, its serious eyes, the respect it awoke in anyone who watched. Nothing like a donkey or a mule. He raised his eyes toward his son: handsome, tall, thin (but for that tendency to put on weight—an endless battle!) and a shadow passed over his face. Why was his heart not content with the glittering joy in David's eyes? Why did he have a bad hunch? He was worried about Ahmed Al-Tal'ooni's cold, penetrating stare. After the match, he came over to shake David's hand. His shake was friendly, sportsmanlike, a hand that had learned from the Brits how to lose gracefully and not hold a grudge, but his eyes, oh, his eyes were of the desert. Blood vengeance, they cried. And who knows if it wasn't by order of the lady, the consul's wife, that he came over with his gesture of camaraderie? Ahmed would not rest. He'd do anything to win back his glory. The Muslim isn't one to give up his honor lightly. Who knew better than Joseph? But it had to be stopped, at all costs. His dream was about to come true. Not through him, but through his son. What's the difference? What he couldn't achieve, his son would, with his assistance. A flame ignited in Joseph's green-hued eyes. A look of clear determination shot a flash of steel through them. He searched for the same sternness in his son's eyes, the one that provides heroes with the glow of glory, but couldn't find it. A dull worry gnawed at his heart. Something of Emilie's refined softness had transferred to their son. He lacked the desire for perfection, and perhaps a masculine pride, without which, how are men better than women? Joseph loved Emilie more than life itself. He always had. Nevertheless, in their early years of marriage, he occasionally tied her to the bed frame and whipped her bare back with his belt, not because of something she'd done, but just to maintain balance, or rather, to maintain the superiority Allah had given man over his wife. Emilie accepted her sentence, because that was the *oossool*, the law of man and nature, and that was how it should be! The Turk is all man. Not like the Egyptian men here. The Turk knows about respect, and loyalty, and love … A deep yearning for Emilie's soft, white skin dulled the daggers of his eyes for a moment. He reached for his son, and as he caressed his face he imagined for a moment that the face was actually his young wife's. He wanted to tie the boy to the bed frame and lash his bare back, but knew that these were new times, and he had to accept them. A foul taste filled his mouth, almost making him sick. Tender ululations sounded from the Arab café on the corner, the divine voice of Umm Kulthum, legendary mother of song, emerging like a ray of light through red clouds … oh, the hookah … the beads … and Umm Kulthum.

Suddenly the clear voice of the godly singer was disrupted by an off-tune screech. An old man in britches and a turban was turning the lever on an organ down in the street, playing some cheap Western tune. A young man in a ratty sailor's uniform broke into a monkey dance to the sounds, and joked nonstop about the monkey's red buttocks. A boy walked among the crowd with a hat in his hand, and once the show was over, solicited tips from the onlookers. Some paid and others refrained. The old man pulled the hat off the sailor's head and raised it toward the balconies. David laughed and threw a few coins down, and the three of them dispersed to collect the ringing treasure, simultaneously bowing.

Joseph wanted to ask his son, "Did you screw her?" but how dare he ask his son such a thing? Let him sleep with her and be done with it! A man should not walk around with pain in his testicles. Especially not a jockey. A jockey mustn't be in love. Love gives you an appetite, and appetite makes you eat—oh, that tendency to put on weight!

Joseph shook his head, and the jolly fringe of his fez moved along with him.

17. IT'S EITHER ME OR …

She let him touch her breasts! They snuck out of the party, squeezed into the Topolino, and even before they went on their way he made a first attempt. She hit his mischievous hand, hard. A nightclub in Bulkeley. Dancing cheek to cheek, so close, eyes almost shut. At the table, in a dark corner, he tried his luck between her thighs. His hand was returned to its place shamefully. Leaving the club, their eyes were on the sea. The full moon brushed silver twinkles along the waves. A languid tango filtered out from the club. He put his arm around her neck, heavy, as if by accident, on her left breast, over the blouse, of course. This first feel went by without a hitch. He squeezed a little, to show her this was no accident, so that she couldn't pretend not to know. She didn't react, only hummed the tango and stared at the moon. He was proud of his achievement. He advanced slowly, already reaching the neckline. From there he could take a sharp turn down toward her skin. His hand continued in its expedition. His excitement grew. His fingertips were already wandering the no-man's-land between the tight brassiere and her soft, supple skin. That smoothness intoxicated him. Suddenly he felt the brash coarseness of the nipple. He was about to shout with joy. The bra wasn't so tight around the nipple, and his fingers had some leeway as they played with the hardening breast.

She was bored, but still expectant. Perhaps a miracle would happen? Someone to take her out of this abysmal boredom, which made her simultaneously indolent and dissatisfied. She would even let him kiss her. Why not? He doesn't smell bad, not even of cigarettes. To him each step was an accomplishment. To her each step was an experiment, an almost desperate attempt at breaking the magic circle. Neither of them was simply enjoying the moment.

Lips touched lips. Tongue touched tongue. His hand still inside her bra. He tried to push the other hand around her back to undo the clasp, but the twisted position they were in hindered his success. Suddenly a Citroën pulled up nearby, and a cheerful group disembarked and proceeded tumultuously right in their direction. Robby's sister detached from him. Damn it, now he'd have to start everything from the beginning. But now she no longer excused his fumbling advances towards her treasures.

He tried being romantic. Sweet nothings, whispers, declarations. He proposed a walk on the deserted beach. There, alone, he'd be victorious. He'd undo her bra if it killed him. Maybe even more than that. The mere thought made him tremble. They strolled on the beach. The moon was shining. She took off her shoes and was suddenly plagued by a deep sadness. Why am I like this? Why can't

I just give myself up to the magic of the moment? Why does everything make me feel contempt? If I didn't think he would get scared, I'd take all my clothes off right now and lie down on the sand for him. This whole thing is so silly.

She couldn't help but compare them, all of them, to her father. Deep down, she felt sorry for David, never thinking to feel sorry for herself.

Suddenly she wanted to have a little fun. She whispered, "Do you want me, David?"

And then, "Do you *really* want me, David?"

The direct question stunned him and he had no words.

She took his hand and put it on her chest, as if saying that this thing he'd been sweating over was the simplest thing in the world. She undid one button of her blouse, to make an easy reach. Her chest moved up and down. She might even have been a bit excited. "Do you want me, David?"

"I ... I'll make you a queen! A queen." This is how David expressed his feelings.

"I'll be yours, David," she said. Then she was scared. Was that it? I'll be yours? So simple? Her breasts were cupped in his hands. The sense of pleasure alarmed her. How did such an explicit promise leave her mouth? Would she keep it, or break it come dawn? She could feel the weight of the threat to her independence, until her lips finally managed to voice that redemptive "if." That "if" that turns the tables.

"If?" His bare feet sank into the sand. He'd been sure the path had been paved straight ahead, and suddenly he was at a crossroads. A choice. He didn't know what to tell her. When she gave her condition, he felt an urge to slap her face. That's what his father would have done. But he couldn't make his hand do that. Since he'd done nothing immediately, he'd missed his chance for a violent response, and had only the path of stuttered words and prolonged silence.

"If you really love me," she chirped, "there should be no question about it." And she redid the buttons of her blouse. David saw her breasts disappearing behind the batiste.

"But why?" he asked. "Why? What does one have to do with the other?"

"It's either me or racing," she repeated, persistent. "Either me or racing either me or racing either me or racing either me or racing ..."

He asked her why again and again, trying to get some answer to put his mind at ease.

"Either-me-or-racing!"

Lilly Elhadeff was prepared to accept him just as he was, while this one asked him to give up his passion, his destiny, his pride, his promising career ... What would he tell his father? He might have given it all up just to get her. Why not? All those cream puffs he was missing out on, all that fat-dripping bacon he couldn't eat because of that damn diet ... If he were a clerk at an insurance company or a cotton marketing firm, or even at the stock market, as his father used to be, before being bitten by the racing bug, he could eat as much as he wanted. He might have given up horse racing and thanked her for rescuing him from the terrible stress, the draining competition, the paralyzing fear of failure—but he knew his father wouldn't stand such a blow. How could he do that to his father?

"It's either me or ..."

And besides, why? Why?

Why? She herself didn't know. Just a momentary impulse. Perhaps a test of his love? Or maybe just an excuse. It was obvious he could not consent to her demands, and this way she could say that he was the one to ruin their chances. And besides, if he did agree to give up this career that set him apart from the anonymous masses just because of the whim of a bored woman who didn't even love him, her contempt would only grow stronger. Why can't she stop comparing them to her father? Would she ever find a man like her father? Ultimately, she thought, Lilly Elhadeff will have David and I'll remain with my yearning for the perfect man, a man who doesn't exist … But how could she give up this independence, this wonderful, intoxicating, dizzying freedom? She enjoyed this game of *femme fatale*, or maybe it was merely her fear of being enslaved to a man, having to play the game for keeps, grow up and become the boring, bored other half of a "*Madame et Monsieur.*" Suddenly she wanted to go home, just to run home and sleep …

"Why?" he kept asking.

"Why? Because I don't want to marry a jockey. A horse is not a stable career, you see? Horses are not a profession, not a future. Horses! Who could live with a man who loves his mare more than his wife? Who could live with a man who weighs himself three times a day? How your mother could have put up with your father, that's her business …"

"Leave my mother out of this, you hear? Leave my mother out of this!" He shook her angrily. What he wouldn't give to break her, she was so fragile, only a woman.

She said coolly, "You're hurting me, Mama's Boy."

"Sorry, I didn't mean to."

"That's just it, *mon ami*, you didn't mean to, but you were ready to whip me. If that's how you're acting now, just think what I have to look forward to once we're married! What can I say, my friend, I want things that … you're a nice boy, but …" Finally she gave up on trying to explain, and summed it up in words he could understand: "I want security, I want money …"

"Money?" David cried and burst out laughing. "That's what you're concerned about? You know how much I made today at the race? You want to know?" and he spat out the amount proudly.

The jingling of coins made a ruckus in her head. That was as much as an average clerk made in six months, she thought with a hint of bitterness and a measure of admiration. She tried to keep cool, maintaining the expression of ridicule.

He added with excitement, "My value on the jockey's stock market, my rating, is rising daily. And my mare, Esperance, also has a high rating. People put their money on us, their savings, their lives. They trust us. *They're* willing to bet on us. Their paychecks, their children's food. *They're* willing to put it all on me, and you're still hesitating?"

He waited silently. She didn't say a word either. She didn't know what to say. She'd never been this close to surrendering. Had he stopped talking that moment, had he grabbed her and kissed her, taking her breath away, crushing her bones and ignoring her stuttering protests, she might have been won over by him. But he was drunk on words, on the bright future filled with money and on the woman he would marry. "If I keep winning like this, I'll be a millionaire!"

"*If* you keep winning!" That was the best response she could muster to his arrogance. All this talk of legendary wealth, of the excitement of betting—win all or lose all—worked its magic. Her eyes glowed a bit, and she looked at him, expecting him to crush her doubt with his strong arms.

Had David not been so self-involved at that moment, he might have noticed that look that said, "Take it all, but do it quickly!" and swept her away. Instead, he continued to glide on the wings of the dream of his own grandeur. "I'm only just beginning, really. They say I have a great future ahead of me. It's all ours. Yours and mine. I'll share it all with you, you get it? We'll go to Europe, to America, to the Far East. The high life! Next summer, when we come back for the racing season, we'll be able to spend the season at the Windsor or the Cecile Hotel – such luxury! We won't have to make do with a meager room at —"

"Like the one you have this summer?"

"Sorry, I didn't mean to offend. The rooms we rented at your place are anything but meager. I like it there. Your place is in an ideal location, walking distance from the track … but you've got to admit, it isn't exactly the Cecile." He laughed arrogantly. His confidence grew as he kept talking, "And there are ways for me to make even *more* money. I can gamble myself. I know which horse and which jockey to put my money on. Ha! True, the rules prohibit it, but between you and me, everybody does it, using a third party. And then, my dear, the sky's the limit!" He took a deep breath and fixed his shimmering eyes on her, as if saying, Now, my fair lady, let's see you say no to this!

"You think I can be bought?" she said coolly, but her voice wasn't as steady as she wanted it to be, which annoyed her.

"Any woman can be bought, baby!" David Hamdi-Ali quoted Humphrey Bogart or Clark Gable.

She burst out laughing, but even her laughter was more hesitant than she'd wanted. Her laughter slowly died down, and she wanted to speak, but didn't know where her words would lead. She'd already decided to gamble, to go with the flow. Wherever it may take her. Her nostrils filled with the smell of the salty breeze, and the moon was low, heavy and ripe. A heaviness also filled her breasts and stomach. She wanted to speak, but was thinking about other things. Her entire body was aware of her feminine blossoming, that wondrous summer bloom that took over young girls, until their lips parted with sweet moisture, and every muscle in their bodies was alert for something … for … "for a wedding, come on!" Grandma would have said impatiently. But this feeling meant freedom, she protested, while a wedding ... she was scared of a wedding, of that constant friction with a stranger, who may see himself entitled to make all sorts of demands, view her as responsible for all sorts of duties, and worst of all—would never change. He'd always be the same man, morning, noon and night. Dancing with the same man, going out with the same man. The same hands caressing her body, maybe even beating it ... She trembled when she recalled her cousin Adele, the eldest daughter of her aunt Tovula, who took a beating from her husband once in a while, and with a belt ... What did she need this for? And why so soon? Especially considering how her parents gave her complete freedom, trusting her judgment, trusting her not to get into trouble. She wouldn't get into trouble, but how about some pleasure? She had to remember, and look out, not let any of them cross that thin, fragile line that separated fun from enslaving devotion. Besides, and maybe this is the main thing, she didn't want to part with her parents, and she missed her brothers in Israel. It might be odd to add this after all this talk of freedom and independence, but she knew she'd never feel better than at her mother's side, and she wasn't ashamed to admit it. But not to David Hamdi-Ali, of course. To him she said only, "What you're saying is very exciting, David, really wonderful, engaging stuff, this horse racing of yours. I can see how important it is to you —"

"To you as well!"

"Much more important to you than I am, and rightfully so!"

"That's not true! You're more important to me than anything in this world!"

"But still you won't give up racing for me."

"You want money, don't you?"

"Money really isn't everything," she said, trying to sound sincere.

"Oh. I'm just so ugly and repulsive that even for my money you wouldn't —"

"Don't be silly. I just can't. It has nothing to do with you."

"Who, then?"

"Me, myself," she said, and couldn't decide if she should tell him the true reason, satisfy his curiosity and show him this was no whim. Yes, it was actually her duty to show him she wasn't simply being spoiled and arbitrary, but that she was facing grave considerations. She had to explain to him that … Suddenly she felt tired. Who said she had to? She didn't owe him a thing! He wanted something, she set a price. The ball was in his court, and she didn't have to reason. He had a decision to make. Deep down, she knew he wouldn't give up racing. No man would humiliate himself that much. Especially seeing how she insisted on not giving him any acceptable reason for her demand, thus making his choice even clearer. "It's either me or racing," she said monotonously, as if nothing he said or did would change that.

David wouldn't give up, but he also seemed tired. They were like two boxers, looking at each other with beaten eyes, going on with the match with an almost mechanical inertia. "But why? Why?"

She walked toward the sea, her feet spraying sand behind her. Her dress clung to her, sending unpleasant chills through her body. She felt the moist sand spraying her. She wanted to take everything off and go into the lukewarm water, but she didn't dare. Not that she was embarrassed to show her body; on the contrary, a mischievous urge to get undressed and tease him pulsed through her. But she was afraid he'd interpret this as an act of love, or surrender.

"Fine, I'll give up racing. I'll give it up, damn it!"

She stopped in her tracks. It couldn't be. This was completely unexpected. She never thought for a moment he might agree. Now the ball was in her court. What would she say? Maybe he was lying. How could she know he would keep his promise? And actually, what did his promise have to do with her? She didn't want him to stop racing. He could keep doing it till the end of time, as far as she was concerned. What now? Plain and simple, set another condition. Would he be willing to leave his country and his family for her, the way his father did for his mother, and follow her wherever she went? This was the pivotal question. But before she even asked it, she made up her mind: she didn't want him to agree to go away with her. She wanted to be free. Even *there*. There, she might explore her future, leaving the past behind. She was young, a little girl, really. She wanted her mommy. What did this stranger want from her? She wanted to say, "Too late!" but knew this was a poor excuse. He'd continue to argue and press her. She didn't want to say anything. She wanted to spread her wings and fly. The dress kept clinging, making her tremble with discomfort. Still, she had to say something, and wasn't sure what.

Luckily, before she could speak, he said, "I'll give it up … after I finish this season."

The fool.

"No," her legs started moving again, leading her into the water. "Starting now, this moment."

"We'll make some money, and then —"

"No!"

"I can't! I can't!" His face was tormented, he was paralyzed and helpless. "I can't do this to him. I can't do it to my father. I just can't." He reached for her hand and said the two words that sealed his fate. "Have mercy."

She took off her clothes, slowly and calmly, as if she were alone in her room, not hiding anything. She wasn't trying to seduce him; he was simply insignificant. That's how Egyptian princesses must have undressed in front of their eunuchs. The wind touched her curves, the sea sprayed white foam in her lap. Light, fast waves swirled around her, caressing her with sounds of explosion, purrs of delight. She closed her eyes and knew that her body was silver and that she was young. Young and free.

He stood on the beach, mouth wide open, not daring to come closer or touch her. "No!" he called out. "I won't give up racing. Who are you to ask me to give anything up? I'll keep going, and I'll be a champion. I'll be rich, and you ... you'll come begging ... yes, on your knees you'll beg me. But I'll tell you to go to hell. I'll tell you, Too late! Too late!" And he walked quickly back to his faithful Topolino.

She barely heard what he'd said, or the sound of the car starting. She was immersed in her delicious surrender to the warm surf.

18. A Letter to Cairo

All the residents saw David the next day as he gave a sealed letter to Salem. The ringing of coins, a gesture of impatience, "Go on, go!" The servant's persistent smile. A master's sigh, accompanied by a hand stuffed into the pocket, another coin for the bakshish, a wide smile, and a slammed door. The echoes of the slamming dispersed like messengers to all corners of the house. Everyone held their breath. Only the ancient grandfather clock ignored the excitement and continued to tick indifferently.

"Did he ask for her hand last night?"

"And if he did, did she say yes?"

"This letter, who is it for and what does it say?"

Grandma was the one to form these three fateful questions. First silently, in her own mind, then later to her daughter, and finally to Emilie Hamdi-Ali. No one had answers.

All morning long, the two protagonists of this drama

locked themselves in their respective rooms. She slept soundly, dreaming about money, more money, and even more money. He sat down to write a letter, with concentration, determination and persistence.

The letter, bearing the portrait of young King Farouk on its top right-hand corner, was on its way. No one could stop it or call it back. Grandma knew that matters had been settled, and there was nothing more for her to do. But she did not know what the verdict had been. She wanted to influence Emilie to get information from her son, but Emilie was taken aback. David could now go back to his room. Silence took over, the echoes of tumult fading. Only curiosity kept creating disquiet, leading to hasty, embarrassed whispering.

"My brother must be screwing your sister," Victor told Robby. Robby kicked his friend in the shin. The kick was retaliated with a slap, the slap led to a scuffle on the carpet, and from the carpet to the tiled floor of the hall, and from there to the hardwood floor of the living room, and back to the balcony.

"What's he doing in there?" Grandma asked Emilie Hamdi-Ali, pointing impatiently toward the door of David's room.

"What's *she* doing in *there*?" Emilie returned the question, pointing to Robby's sister's room.

"She's sleeping. She's always sleeping."

"What does that mean? Is that a sign?"

"It's no sign, I'm telling you, when is she ever awake? The whole world can burn down, but she—*papeyando!*"

They both sighed. The coffee arrived and they shook their heads, taking loud sips. Suddenly they paused. While the porcelain rattled and some drops flew out, they sat frozen. David's door opened and he appeared in his white tennis clothes, handsome as a Hollywood dream. The old ladies were shaken and couldn't take their eyes off him as he walked measuredly and proud, scaring off the darkness of the hall. Emilie looked at her son with gratitude for how handsome and tall he was, as if this were how he repaid her for all she'd done for him. "God save him, amen."

Grandma could not ignore this generous, glowing beauty either, and could not hold back a mumble of excitement: "*Como un Americano.*"

A smile of satisfaction spread over Emilie's lips, sending waves of happiness through her body. With her natural sensuality, which had not faded with the years, this wave translated into passion for her husband, whose impressive masculine ugliness was so different than her son's bright, somewhat feminine attractiveness.

Grandma felt certain that David's ceremonial appearance would be accompanied by a formal announcement, "I'm glad to tell you, good women ..."

Or: "I've been silent so far, because I wasn't able to express my joy in words ..."

Or: "Why should I keep you in suspense? Well ..."

But not a word left his mouth. With measured steps he walked to the middle of the hall and began his workout ritual. That same introverted look. Only David Hamdi-Ali existed in the world in those moments. Only him—his body, his soul, his eyes, his ears, his nose, his chest, his arms, his legs and ... oh, that too ... that too ... a dull ache sent waves down to his testicles. He bit his lips, pulled himself together and continued—one, two, three, right! One, two, three, left!

It was clear the sphinx wasn't going to deliver.

Suddenly Salem appeared, sprouting all of a sudden from the shadows, as was his manner. David gave him an inquisitive look which Salem returned: mission accomplished, *ya sidi*! A vague smile graced David's face. A bit of vengeance, a bit of pride, a bit of depression. A sleepless night afforded his cheeks a sickly pallor that only added a soft transparency to his beauty. An ecstatic satisfaction reflected in his motions.

The letter was on its way. Now no one could stop it or call it back. Not even him. The matter had been settled. Finally.

Grandma cornered Salem in the kitchen and asked, "Where is the letter going?"

"The post office," said Salem sneakily.

"Don't be an ass. I know you took it to the post office, but to whom is it addressed?"

"Oh, to whom is it addressed, you should say that's what you mean, Madame."

"Fine, I said it. Well?"

"How should I know, Madame? Mister Hamdi-Ali didn't tell me."

"And you didn't look at the envelope, huh? Don't play games!"

"Since when can I read *Françaoui*?" Salem said innocently, a sweet smile on his face.

Grandma realized that only bakshish would make him talk. She did what she had to do and the answer soon arrived.

"*Al-Cahira*."

"To whom exactly in Cairo?"

Another bit of bakshish and all the information was revealed, just like in those American machines all over town: you put in a piaster and it gives you your weight. They say there are even machines that tell you your future. Grandma shelled out some cash and the prophecy was sounded: "To a certain Lilly Elhadeff."

It seemed that it was all over. All was lost. But Grandma's mind never stopped working. New questions were posed with amazing speed, matching the changing circumstances:

Did he write to ask for her hand?

If so, will she say yes?

Or perhaps he wrote to break it off?

Everything was still open. Grandma was exhausted and enraged. The audacity of youth, never considering their benefactors' right to know!

Robby's mother claimed that had the news been good, David would have already shared it.

19. LILLY MON AMOUR

"Lilly Mon Amour,

You must be surprised to receive this letter after such a long silence. First I must apologize for not answering your four letters. The truth is, I wanted to write you, but I was very busy preparing for the race. Yesterday was the big day. You probably read in *Le Progrès Egyptien* that our wonderful Esperance did not let us down and brought me in at first place. My old man was pleased and proud, as was I. Only one thing clouded my joy—that you, *ma chère* Lilly, were not there. Oh, how complete my joy would have been if it were accompanied by a kiss from your lips, my dear. You'll probably say: if you wanted me so badly, you would have bothered to write or call! To this (if you do say it) I have only one answer: the fear, *ma chère* Lilly, that I might lose the race and let you down, the shame that would have gnawed at me had that been the case, they made it comfortable for me not to have you there. Had I known for certain that I'd win, would I ever give up the company of my fiancée?

"No, *chérie*, that is no mistake. I've made up my mind: I am hereby asking for your hand in marriage. Try to imagine David Hamdi-Ali getting down on his knees and reciting a poem. If you say yes, we'll get married in the fall, at the end of the season, immediately upon our return from Alexandria. You'll probably ask what motivated me to decide and act all of a sudden. First, I would have to correct you: it isn't all of a sudden. Not at all. I've always loved you. The decision to ask you to marry me became more firm in my heart during these days when I missed you so much. Maybe it's the air here, the sea air, which makes me yearn. Alexandria is intoxicating, but I think it brings out the best in me, and the best in me is my love for you. I miss you, Lilly, my little Lilly, I miss your smile and your eyes, your hair and other parts that I don't want to mention in writing, should your mother find this letter ...

"Had I not been so busy all week long with preparations and training, and on weekends with the races themselves, I would fly straight to Cairo and take you in my arms. But there's no chance I can leave in the next few weeks. Maybe you can come this weekend? There's nothing in the world that would make me happier or prouder. You'd be my lucky charm for the next race. I'll make you a queen ..."

And so on and so forth, a long letter full of tired repetitions. David was proud of the web of small lies he'd patiently and carefully woven. He'd come up with a vicious idea and had executed it in a cold and calculated way. It was clear he had no intention of keeping his promise. He was merely getting back at Lilly for what Robby's sister had done. And maybe he was getting back at Robby's sister as well. Could he make her jealous? Would he be that successful?

David got carried away with these thoughts for a few moments longer, until suddenly, with a kind of determination, he shook both women off and sent them to hell. Women! We mustn't let them drain us of our power and take over our thoughts. This is a man's world. Men, two men, face-to-face on the track. While the horses gallop as fast as the wind and your head spins with effort, all the women in the world fade away. Only the two of them remain. Two men: he, David, the Jew, against the dark desert man. The other jockeys exist only on paper, but their presence is eliminated on the track, and only they remain—he and Al-Tal'ooni.

I can't let him win even once, David thought. I can't let that Arab beat me. Besides, I have to win so I can prove to everybody, and especially to her, that this has no effect on me whatsoever. He looked at her closed door with hatred. Sleeping soundly, as if nothing happened. I couldn't sleep at all last night.

Suddenly he had a strong urge for a baba au rhum. That sweet, spongy cake, nauseatingly covered with thick whipped cream, and over that a glassy coat of caramel that shatters between your teeth.

She wolfed down two of those at the Nautical Club, with that charming nonchalance. He sat there, mad with envy, but he resisted. Yes, he resisted! But now the urge to gorge was desperately strong. Had someone served him that lethal pastry right this moment, he doubted he could hold back.

Luckily, no devil came bearing baked goods, and his desire waned, and only a vague and indescribable yearning remained.

Nevertheless, when he weighed himself an hour later, the scales showed he'd gained half a kilo.

"Half a kilo!" David couldn't believe his eyes. He'd been so careful with that damn diet.

His father approached and David quickly jumped off the scales before he could catch him in this moment of weakness.

"How much?" Joseph asked routinely.

David lied, cutting a few grams off from the previous weigh-in. Joseph was pleased and David felt guilty. He was afraid his father would ask him to get back on the scale again, but he needn't have worried. Not a shadow of a doubt clouded Joseph's sunny face, and he patted his son on the shoulder and said in English, "Good boy, good boy!"

David felt even more ashamed. He swore not to eat a thing until the next weigh-in.

The fast was hard and nerve-wracking, especially following a sleepless night. He counted the hours and the minutes before his next weigh-in. His body rebelled: Why did he set the next weigh-in for so late? Who said he couldn't do it half an hour, or even an hour earlier? Perhaps he should wait only until the first star appears or until the shofar is blown, like on Yom Kippur? But David didn't give in to these delusions, and bravely maintained the fast he'd punished himself with. He wouldn't cheat, even by one minute. He'd even wait a few minutes longer, just to be sure. He tried to sleep, but the hunger wouldn't leave him alone. He lay in bed, in a state of tortured serenity, and saw himself as a sort of fakir or dervish. Or perhaps a prophet or a monk.

His mother came in and wanted to know if he was ill, God forbid. She wasn't used to seeing him lying in bed in the middle of the day, a strange smile on his face.

"No! I'm not ill. I feel great!" And to prove it, he jumped out of bed. For a moment he felt like his head would fall off, as if his dizziness created such a strong centrifugal force that it would spin off his neck, but he grabbed the round brass ornament on the bed frame and the coolness of the metal felt good, and before his mother became truly alarmed, he managed a smile.

"You haven't eaten a thing all day." Her tone was concerned and accusatory at once. Not eating was a sin as far as she was concerned.

"Yes I have."

"No you haven't. Come, I'll make you two eggs, just the way you like them, fried in butter. Salem just brought fresh baguettes."

"No!" he said, alarmed. The two eggs appeared in his mind, two gaping sickly-yellow eyes. "No!" That half a kilo weighed down like a burden on his heart.

"You're sick, I'll call a doctor."

"Don't call a doctor, Mama. Do me a favor, Mama, and don't call a doctor. All I need is to be left alone for a while!" He tried to tame his anger, raising his voice only a bit, but it was enough to break her dam of tears.

"Do you have a hand … hand … handkerchief?"

Why is she doing this to me? His handsome face, under the delicate makeup of suffering, wandered the room and caught its own reflection in the mirror over the vanity table. A close-up sprinkled with the sun's golden powder. Without taking his eyes off his reflection, he handed his mother his spotless white handkerchief and muttered some weak words of solace, watching his lips move as if on their own, detached from the words they were uttering. Deep in his heart he resented having to comfort his mother while he was himself sunk in desperation. Suddenly he saw her face in the mirror, the face of an old lady. David was shocked. It was the first time his mother had become diminished to him, as if thrown off her throne as her chosen son stood to the side, never lending a hand. The throne appeared empty and he almost felt desolate, but then he saw Robby's sister, dressed in the see-through chiffon of stardust, rising to sit upon the throne. His self-pity grew, and with it his rage and helplessness. Distress suffocated him and he didn't know where to turn. Luckily, his younger brother, Victor, walked into the room, playing a harmonica: it felt like a saw slicing into his flesh.

"Cut out that noise!!!" David screamed, grabbing his brother and pummeling him.

The storm helped clear his soul, and brought a sort of relief to David, who could breathe again. Victor gagged and wept like a wounded animal.

"David, David, what's wrong with you?" his mother asked, scared.

"Mama," he said, elated, "I'll eat your fried eggs!"

Emilie raised her eyes to the sky and thanked the good

Lord. As long as people are eating … "Come, Victorico, I'll make you two fried eggs as well."

After eating and praising his mother, David snuck into the bathroom, shoved two fingers up his throat and returned the meal to the sewers. Now he was pleased: he'd appeased his mother without damaging his diet. Knowingly and maliciously he'd betrayed his mother's trust, but his heart was light and he was relieved, happy and proud. His asceticism made his limbs feel lighter, as if he was stepping out of his body. His head floated among the clouds, and he was assured his body was as weightless as a cloud in a summer sky.

Esperance will even be surprised at how light I am, he thought, and hopped onto the scale.

One-hundred-and-seventy grams more than the previous weigh-in! It was maddening! Maddening! What was causing this?

The main thing was to keep his secret. Things would work out in the end. David was a natural optimist and believed that God loved him. Robby's sister might not love him, but who was she compared to God?

The sun invaded the house, sweeping up its dark corners and almost reaching the depths of the hall with its frantic, curious rummaging. The rattle of copper sounded from the street. An old Arab man, wearing a skullcap, dragging loose britches between his legs like a sort of forgotten placenta, carried a plump sack on his shoulder that rang like the bells of ten churches. He called at the top of his lungs, "*Nahàss! Nahàss!*"

All the housewives sent down their servants with pots and pans, and the old man put them in his sack. For a small fee, this patina-stricken crockery would be returned to its owners glowing a bright gold. From the balcony, Robby could see all the cauldrons flowing into the sack, and yet the sack was never full, and the old man did not collapse under the burden.

"Nahàss! Nahàss!"

A piece of copper flashed through a hole in the sack, winking at the sun. The sack was full of cheerful suns.

"God loves me," said David, indulging himself once more in his reflection in the hall mirror. In it, he saw the reflection of a painting that hung on the opposite wall. A cloudy, pastoral landscape. Green-brown trees, a herd of sheep grazing in the meadow, a pointy-eared dog, alert and prepared to give his life for any of the sheep, never imagining that the bone he receives as his reward at the end of each day came from the body of one of these woolly beasts, living for a moment in the dewy green, knowing nothing of slaughterhouses. A strange, nostalgic European landscape that David had only ever seen in movies or in textbooks in French class. The *paravent* also reflected in the mirror, a screen not intended to hide anything— a decoration meant merely to please the eye. Across the black fabric, an embroidered peacock spread its gorgeous feathers. Until that moment, David had never given any thought to this peacock. Now it seemed to have been born from darkness just for him, to expand his mind, a sign of grace, a sign of good things to come. They say Robby's grandmother embroidered that peacock when she was a young girl, perhaps even back in Turkey. Strange to think that the old lady was able to produce such a masterpiece. She can barely read or write, but she has a sense of humor, that old bag, and she ... she wants me so badly to marry her granddaughter. Perhaps I should just explain to her ... frankly, without excuses, why I finally decided not to marry her ...

Now David believed that he'd been in control of the entire matter from the start, and if he was engaged to Lilly Elhadeff rather than to Robby's sister, that meant this was his desire and his choosing. The face in the mirror, the delicate, fair features, spread light over the glass. He could sit like this for hours, stroking his eyes over his reflection, studying each feature, trying to crack his own puzzle, as if the sphinx itself were smiling from the mirror. Suddenly he truly pitied Robby's sister. If she could only open her eyes and see what she was missing! That Lilly Elhadeff, that smiling skeleton, she'll win the jackpot, it's practically being forfeited to her. He sighed, still believing deep in his heart that a loving hand was guiding the world, and his life especially.

His mother's reflection appeared in the mirror. David looked at fat Emilie and was appalled. His confidence in himself had been shaken: he could see his career sinking into a pit of fat, drowning in it with a gurgle. He'd inherited the curse of weight from her. A trickle of hate toward her suddenly dripped inside his heart, as if by her mere existence she'd sentenced the jockey David Hamdi-Ali to failure.

"Emilie isn't fat."

"She isn't thin either, is she?"

"Chubby. As they say *en français*, *potelée*," Robby's grandmother said.

"*Potelée* or not, it certainly doesn't become her."

"I think it looks nice. The Turks have always preferred their women with a little cushion, not like those skeletons walking around today with a boy's haircut!"

Who can argue with Grandma when she gets her evidence from the Turks?

Madame Marika, whose own size was way beyond what was fashionable, could not comprehend why everyone was so understanding of Emilie's figure, even going so far as to point out her loveliness, while her own figure inspired nothing but ridicule and wrinkled noses. She'd always carried her extra weight as a sort of protest, but this wasn't to say that she didn't feel wronged and persecuted. The cascades of fat had been part of her life ever since she was a little girl in Izmir. True, Turkish men do like chubby women, Madame Marika thought, but nobody liked fat women. Tears of rage rose in her throat, but then she remembered her husband, Vita, her skinny, modest Vita, whose weight she could barely feel the first time he climbed, like a long-limbed cricket, atop her voluptuous belly. She felt a sort of tickle back then, and almost laughed, but resisted, knowing that was no way to treat a man as he, breathing heavily, mounted the woman he'd married that very day. Vita was prepared to accept her just as she was, along with the considerable dowry her widower father had paid. But that was long ago. Since then they've had Eliyo, Becky, Julia, Rose and Nissimiko, whom they sometimes called Nisimachi, as was the Turkish manner, and counting. Renée Marika felt a little better and was ready to go to battle.

"What's for sure is that David's wife won't be fat. Not even *potelée*." Madame Marika giggled. "She'll be skinny *como un palo*!"

"You're saying my granddaughter is skinny as a stick?" Grandma asked innocently.

"Who's talking about your granddaughter?" Madame Marika laughed maliciously. "You know Fortunée Elhadeff?"

"Of the Cairo Elhadeffs?" Grandma pretended not to know what this was about.

"Of the Cairo Elhadeffs," Marika confirmed. "From Heliopolis."

"Of course I know her," Grandma said and could not contain a heavy sigh.

"Fortunée has a daughter." Meaningful pause. "Did I say skinny *como un palo*? No, skinnier than that. Skinny *como un fideio*, a noodle."

"What's that got to do with David?"

"Here's Emilie Hamdi-Ali in the flesh. Why don't you ask her if what I'm saying isn't true?"

"What isn't true?" said Emilie with her familiar

innocence.

"It isn't true? Who says it isn't true?" Marika cried. "I keep saying it is true, that your little David is going to marry *la cocona d'Elhadeff.*"

Silence. The buzzing of afternoon flies filled the summer air, along with the heavy breathing of the women, shocked by the words that had been spoken. Fateful words, an irreversible verdict. Alexandria could not handle such explicitness. What you don't talk about doesn't hurt so much, you can turn a blind eye, pretend it never happened. But an explicit word sends waves through the peaceful standing water ...

Grandma could not focus on rummy at all that day. Even the joker, with his cheeky smile, could not cheer her up.

20. A GREAT, RARE BLESSING

During the next Kudjoocome, Grandma cornered Robby's sister and demanded an explanation.

Robby's father told her off, "*No té mesklés,* don't intervene!"

"*Ma porqué?*" Grandma protested. "Why not? Aren't we human beings? Don't we deserve answers? Shouldn't she explain herself to her mother?"

"She's almost twenty years old. She knows what she's doing." Then he added, hiding a smile, "I hope."

"What do you think, Papa? Should I marry David?"

This direct question upset him. She was asking for a clear answer, real advice. Robby's father didn't put much stake in advice. One never asks for someone else's advice before having already made up his mind, wanting nothing more than support for his decision, a confirmation that contributes nothing. He sighed. What should he tell her? Did he even know David Hamdi-Ali? He'd barely spoken to him since his family moved in. Just a few nods. Nevertheless, Robby's father knew for certain that Hamdi-Ali junior was a superficial boy, not too bright. Robby's father never had much patience for fools. As it turned out, he did have an opinion in the matter. The girl acted wisely, turning David down. Still, he was comfortable not voicing his opinion, not having the matter discussed in a family forum. If this forum began discussing all the romantic involvements of his children, what would be the end of that?

Everyone waited for him to speak. No one dared urge him, not even Grandma.

Finally he sighed and said, "*I* wouldn't marry David Hamdi-Ali."

The oracle had spoken. The matter was settled. A short, clear-cut answer. Robby's sister looked at her father gratefully. Their eyes met. A hint of a smile drained into the corners of his eyes, and she returned the favor with a wide smile of her own. They understood each other. How great the distance was between David's loud arrogance and her father's confident quiet, which contained endless fountains of wisdom. She adored him and vowed to only ever marry a man who would measure up to him. Her eyes wandered over to her mother's good, slightly plump face. She was so attached to these people! They were both still in the prime of their lives, but she knew it wouldn't be long before their hair turned silver. Wrinkles would appear on her mother's smooth face, the skin of which was taut and rosy, especially after the siesta. The thought was too sad and she wanted to cry, but was afraid that her grandmother might interpret her tears as a lament for the end of her affair with David Hamdi-Ali. Grandma's skin had already yellowed slightly, and age spots had spread over her concave forehead. Her green eyes, quick and stubborn, stuck out of deepening sockets. She loved Grandma. They'd always had a secret bond, in spite of their constant bickering. She must know that this wasn't merely a whim. This was too serious a matter. Robby's sister decided at once to break her vow of silence, and spoke.

Grandma was shocked. She was under the impression that her granddaughter had rejected David due to frivolity. Now this *cocona* was giving her a list of thought-out reasons she could barely stand to deny. This one most of all:

"The boys are in Israel. Papa said that sooner or later we'll all join them. David would never go to Israel. There are no horse races there, and his father wouldn't let him give up horse racing. David isn't one to disobey his father, and even if he were, what would he do then? This way he has money, he has fame. Without horse racing, what would he be worth? There's no chance he'll ever leave Egypt. I don't want to be away from you. You're more important to me than all the Hamdi-Alis in the world. I also don't want all of us to stay here because of me, far away from the boys ..."

"As Jews, our only future is in Israel," her father confirmed. His view on this matter was clear. He'd never been an active, militant Zionist, like his friend and neighbor Maurice Rosenberg, who'd already served several months in an Egyptian prison for underground Zionist activity. Robby's father did not like politics. He preferred to read a novel, not a newspaper, and hardly listened to the news on the radio. A few months prior, his second son wrote him from his training in France, telling him he had received an offer to stay and become a French citizen, thanks to his excellence on the local basketball team. He asked for his father's advice. His father did not hesitate and instructed him to turn down the offer and continue to Israel, and his son did, along with his older brother. In spite of their independence, or perhaps because of their independence, the children cherished their father's opinion, never underestimating it.

"I don't want to be away from you," Robby's sister said and gave her father a long kiss. Robby jumped up and kissed her. A united family, what a great, rare blessing.

21. *YALLA, YA IBNI*, LET'S GO, MY SON!

On Wednesday afternoon, David got up and drove to one of the big stores on Rue Cherif Pacha to buy a new scale. He ordered his mother to sell the old one, which was without a doubt the cause of his bad luck, to the *roba bequia*—an Arabic distortion of *Roppa Vequia*, old rags, the old man walking the city and purchasing used goods, who was often the subject of legends about the wealth he'd accumulated through years of buying and selling rags.

The new scale was kind to David. His weight did not diminish, but neither did it rise, and he wholeheartedly believed that a crisis had been averted. Perhaps it was even a good omen, and his weight would drop in the few days that remained before the next race.

He tripled and quadrupled his workout sessions, and spent several hours each day riding on the track, while his old father circled him with satisfaction, wearing a jacket over his bright white shirt, the fez never leaving his head.

"My son is back with me. My son is back with us," he mumbled to himself, his eyes sparkling.

On the night before the race he told David, "Go get dressed, *ya ibni*. We're going out."

"Going out? Where?"

"Out, I said. Out. Just you and I. Let's go, go on, get dressed."

"What about Mama?"

"Just you and I, I said." He asserted his oriental authority, and David didn't dream of protesting. He went to his room to carry out orders.

The old man remained in the hall on his own. From

the room at the end of the hall he vaguely heard the chattering of the women playing their game of rummy, which they all called *cuncan*.

Cuncan, cuncan, he thought with distaste and sighed. The women here are too liberated, as are the men. He pulled his prayer beads from his pocket and slowly rolled them around between his fingers. It would be best if Emilie avoided that cuncan—it slowed the brain and corrupted the morals. At first he was going to forbid it, but then he took pity on her and thought, if she likes it so much, let her play. What pleasure does a woman have in her life, and in her old age, no less? As was the case whenever he thought of his Emilie, a wave of love swept up his old body, which yearned for rest at the end of the road more than it craved the excitement of the moment.

Secret passions evolved with time and congealed into memories. The silhouette of Leila, the mare, rose against his tired eyes. Noble, black, agile, sleek Leila; perfect Leila, who would never grow old. Emilie is so different, the very opposite. Leila was black and Emilie is white, Leila was skinny and Emilie—round, Leila was all muscle, taut as a string, while Emilie's flesh is soft, soft and delicate to the touch. Nevertheless, at times the two become fused in his mind. His love makes them one. And maybe it also had to do with that wild look in their eyes, Leila's and Emilie's. But Leila was truly wild, while Emilie's sole wildness is in her eyes, the rest of her soft and gentle as a ewe. What would he ever do without her? When Leila died, in that strange, faraway city, he was like one of the old man's rags. Another woman might have said, she was only a mare (*only* a mare!); but Emilie said nothing. Did she understand him in his tragedy? Or was she simply sensible enough and loving enough to do the right thing and leave him be, letting his grief ripen until it fell away by itself, like fruit from a tree? Or maybe she was just crudely indifferent to his fate? No, not at all. Perhaps she was lazy? Perhaps. Perhaps she was embarrassed or at a loss? Perhaps. The important thing is what she did. The important thing is, she did not force herself on him, did not make any cheap attempts to fill the void left by Leila. Emilie was one thing, and Leila was another. Each had her own special place. When one left, her absence was never filled. The old man closed his eyes and saw this black void, this emptiness, this eternity.

The beads slipped between his fingers, the touch of the cold amber making him feel peaceful. A light nap. Was this death? An old man, falling asleep in the afternoon sun, his eyes closed, his mouth open, his fingers spreading by themselves and the beads slowly falling to the carpet.

David stood before him in a sharkskin suit, white as the angel Gabriel when he showed himself to Muhammad, white as the fresh morning, blessed by Allah with a rejuvenating breeze from the sea.

Joseph shook off the sleep and bits of dream. He stood up, encouraged, and linked his arm with his son's, whispering in his ear: "*Yalla, ya ibni.*"

22. *UNE P.*

Victor and Robby stood on the balcony, their chins pressed against their arms on the cool stone and the rough, peeling plaster. They watched the two men moving away up the street: a tall young man, blinding white, his blond hair reflecting the rays of the sun as they lingered on the brilliantine; a firm but slightly hunched older man, wearing black, a red fez burning atop his head in the afternoon sun.

"Do you know where he's taking him?" Victor whispered in Robby's ear, his breath hot and sticky. He did not wait for an answer and added, "To *une P.*" Robby's eyes told him the hint was insufficient, and so he elaborated: "*Une prostituée.*"

Robby had never heard that word, but his heart told him that it's meaning lay in those moldy, mysterious corners, in the appealing, frightening world of sex. Plug your ears, hear no more. But every cell in his body thirsted for more knowledge. In a strange voice he asked, "What's that?"

Victor's laugh resounded like a pile of empty cans tumbling down from the balcony.

Robby regretted asking. Once more he was dragged in spite of himself into a dangerous zone. He wanted to take it back. In his mind's eye, he once more saw his parents walking around naked, cheerfully playing games that were not suitable for adults. He hated Victor Hamdi-Ali so. Hated him and waited, waited impatiently for his words.

"A prostitute is a woman who screws for money."

"People *pay* for it?"

"You bet."

"I don't believe you."

"You don't believe me. Fine, don't believe me. But there are houses like that, there are. You go there, walk in, pay, then they put you in a room where a woman waits for you, totally naked. You take your clothes off and screw her. After you finish, you pay and leave. It's simple."

Robby looked back at the two men walking away. "What! You mean to tell me that your father is taking your brother to a woman like that?"

"Shh … the whole house will hear you."

"It can't be!"

"You're an idiot. What do you know, anyway? You're a baby." He turned his back on him with ridicule.

A father taking his son to a prostitute. Would his father also come to him one day and say, "Robby, let's go," then take him by the hand to a big, dark house? What do those houses look like? Maybe they're more like palaces? Rooms upon rooms, like cells in a beehive. In each cell, a naked woman. His father would motion and say, "Choose, son, the world is your oyster," twisting his face with a small, lusty smile. The whole world is gaping, pink genitalia. He wouldn't know what to do. His eyes would cling to his father for help. Once he almost drowned in a whirlpool in the capricious sea, in the Agami neighborhood, and thought his end was nigh, but then he felt his father's arm grab him, ripping him away from the water's death grip. This time, however, his father would not come to his aid. On the contrary, he'd say, "That's it, from here on out, you're on your own." On his own in a small, seedy room with cobwebs and … a woman. A big, writhing woman, a womb of quicksand …

"But … why?"

Victor smiled and hugged him almost paternally. "So that he can let go of all that tension. So he can be light for his race, and win."

A simple, satisfying explanation. Emotional pressure. Stress and nervousness before his race. A bit of entertainment (apparently, going to a prostitute is somewhat entertaining) can help release such tensions. Robby never imagined that such a release could be a basic, simple, physiological process, just like squeezing toothpaste out of the tube, and inquired no further. Not that he had all the answers now, but the serenity of the afternoon made him feel languid and sleepy. The sun sprawled out among the clouds, like a giant orange on a pile of white blankets. A light breeze caressed tired eyelids.

At the Café de la Paix, old men and women in summer garb began taking over the round white tables scattered over the sidewalk, their large, colorful sun umbrellas unable to protect the diners from the warm, diagonal rays. The elderly breathe in the wind and, with half-shut eyes, sip their Turkish coffee with creamy brown kaimak on top. Among them is a young couple, their faces tan and their arms bare, a floral dress with a cheeky neckline. A throaty voice bubbles up, like the cooing of pigeons in love. An Arab selling jasmine wreaths enters. Multiple flower necklaces hang from his neck and arms, and he pushes a reed cart full of them. From the height of the second floor, Robby becomes intoxicated with the aroma of flowers, or maybe it is his imagination, not his nose, that enjoys the scent. The young man buys some wreaths and wraps them around his girl's neck. She laughs, her bouncing chest spraying off shreds of flowers, and the white of the jasmine sprays like sea foam over tanned curves. Waves of perfume rise again with a light wind. The breath is calm. The eyes close.

David sat slightly apart from the rest. From within the cloud of heavy smoke, illuminated by the red lights of the club, his father's fez appeared again, red hot, like the floating barrel that bobbed among the waves at Sporting Beach. At his side were several other fezzes—the old men spoke emphatically, their faces businesslike and their wrinkles vibrating. With dreamy, covetous eyes, David watched the frantic curves of the dancer Shakra Roomy. Her twitching navel hypnotized him into intoxication. Her protesting breasts, demanding to remove the burden of the golden brassiere, decorated with glass necklaces and jingling coins, also swirled in circles through the air, and in a moment of delusion he imagined them rubbing his burning face. The *raki*, that Turkish anise spirit, diluted with a drop of water, created hot steam inside his head, thickening clouds of fog before him, and through it all, the sounds of rhythmic eastern music, going round and round in endless cadence ... In his blurry mind, David wondered if the girl had a price. He was once told that every woman had a price, but, in his natural decency, refused to believe it. Women like his mother, for instance, could not be bought. Suddenly it occurred to him that women like Robby's sister could not be bought either, and the thought sobered him, like a broom sweeping away the cobwebs of merciful drunkenness. He quickly brushed the thought away and returned to his expedition around Shakra Roomy's jiggling belly.

Shakra wasn't an Arab. Her parents had migrated to Alexandria from the Balkans, possibly in the same period that Joseph and Emilie Hamdi-Ali and Robby's parents arrived as well. David once read a book, perhaps by the great Flaubert, a travel book about 19th century Egypt, in which Turkish belly dancers, who in Egypt served as high-end prostitutes, shaved the pubic hair off their romantic triangle. The thought sent a tremble of lust through him. A woman, white from head to toe (in his excitement he forgot the brownish-pink halos around her nipples), a little girl, blown-up. He'd often seen little girls in the nude. In his virginal imagination, he tried to illustrate this metamorphosis, but he couldn't conjure up a clear image of a shaved woman, which served only to further ignite his elusive lust. This Shakra must also have a price. Distractedly, he rummaged through his pockets, feeling some bills and coins. Had his father not been with him, he would have tried to discuss a more intimate meeting with her. He looked at his father, and though the latter was conversing with the other men and paying no attention to his son's endeavors, David blushed and curled up in his corner.

"Hamdi-Ali, *ya omri*, my soul!" one fat Armenian in a fez tried sweet-talking Joseph. "*Ya* Hamdi-Ali, my brother, who knows better than you that the God above gives only one chance, whether you're a wise man or a fool, you only get one. The wise man jumps at it, grabbing it like … like a woman's breasts. While the fool …" He waved the thought away.

Joseph said nothing. His eyes were dark and stubborn. Once in a while, he glanced at his son, glad that David wasn't listening to this shameful conversation he was forced to have with his friends. His friends! One trainer and two bookies. The trainer, his old Greek friend, Panayotti Helikos, who'd been Ahmed Al-Tal'ooni's trainer and business manager for a long time. He was a small man, with a shiny black mane and a hooked mustache that looked as if it were painted over his thin top lip with pencil liner. He spoke with exhausting speed, switching languages to create a mélange of Turkish, Greek, French and Arabic, with a few English words to spice things up. With his will of steel, he'd decided to turn his employer into a champion, no matter what, even recruiting the support of the two craftiest bookmakers in Alexandria, the Armenian twins, Toto and Sisso Georgian.

How dire, that Joseph was forced to sit here, at his age, with his flawless reputation, like a city under siege, suffocated with smoke, attacked from all directions. He wanted to go out to the night air, stand by himself, lean beneath the yellow glow of a streetlamp and smoke his cigarette quietly, *his* cigarette alone, inhaling only its smoke, without the nauseating mixture of smoke and hot breath, turning the air inside the club into an unbearable mush. The repetitive rhythmic music, looping endlessly, pounded inside his head like a stubborn hammer.

For a moment, he thought he was going to have a heart attack: sudden suffocation, grotesque spasms, his eyes popping out of their holes, panic ... doctor! Is there a doctor in the house?

He gritted his teeth and prayed it wasn't happening to him. Not here, not here, surrounded by his so-called friends, Panayotti, Toto and Sisso, the three men he'd joined countless times in this club so favored by the racing industry. He'd often joked around with them, enjoying their company, and truly thought they were his close friends. But Joseph Hamdi-Ali never had true friends, and therefore had no point of reference.

Toto worked him with his slick tongue, and then Pan-ayotti tried his luck with quick rhetoric, and finally Sisso delivered a short series of threats. But Joseph was firm in his opinion—not for all the money in the world.

The three men saw this as an invitation to raise their offer. They exchanged quick looks of consultation, a crooked smile to signal that every man had his price, and righteous Joseph was no exception. Toto named a higher price than before. Joseph chuckled and said, "No!" They could not believe that modest, bashful Joseph, whom they thought of as a simple, naive lamb, dared demand a higher price than they'd offered, and never imagined that here was a gullible man, honest to the point of boredom, who could not be tempted with money.

Joseph laughed silently. He thought: my son must be a real star if these three vultures, may their names and memories be wiped from eternity, are willing to pay, and in advance, no less, so certain are they that my son is going to win. Thank you for the vote of confidence, gentlemen!

While he pondered this, he heard Panayotti name a new, dizzying price. Joseph pictured hundreds of Egyptian pound notes swirling through the wind in front of his tired eyes. He hoped with all his heart that David heard nothing. He could not guess his son's reaction to such an offer.

Luckily, David's eyes were captivated by the charms of the beautiful, snow-white odalisque. The Turks like ivory flesh. Joseph looked at him, then at her, and thought, why not? His son wants her, and he shall get her, no matter the price. David is a prince, and a prince deserves it all. This was also a chance to escape from the three predators and their shameful offer. He waved over to the waiter, his old friend, a Maltese man with a quiet face and a paternal look, gestured toward Shakra and asked, "How much?"

The Maltese shook his head as if to say, You couldn't afford it, *ya ahi*, these kind of goods are for the pashas and the *beys* and the diplomats.

But Joseph insisted, and a price was named. "Does she take checks?"

"From you, *ya sidi*, certainly."

"Let's go, *ya ibni*," said Hamdi-Ali, dragging along his amazed son.

23. IVANHOE

The next day was the day of the race.

The entire household was in attendance, except for Robby and Victor, of course. Even Salem went, wearing his Sunday best, a calm and solemn expression on his face. As did the Murad sisters, in new dresses and wide-brimmed straw hats, laughing ceaselessly. Only Robby's sister didn't take part in the excitement. Early in the morning, before the rest of the house woke up, she left for a picnic and a bicycle ride in the Nuzha Gardens with Maître Ramzi.

The teasing began:

"Since when does that *cocona* wake up so early in the morning?"

"The power of love!"

"Just don't let her get attached. A Christian!"

"Not Christian, Coptic," Grandma corrected, but deep inside she knew the difference was insignificant.

"The Copts are Christian."

"The Greeks are Christian!"

"So what are the Copts?"

"Copts."

"Christian or Copt, they're all the same—they do not love the Jews!"

"Shh, watch your tongue, Madame Marika. Madame Murad might hear you …"

They all left the house and flocked to the sidewalk. The sounds of chatter rose to the sky. Robby and Victor were home alone. The slamming of the doors still echoed through the hall, mixing with the ticking of the grandfather clock.

Without a word, the two of them dropped their pants and began rolling around on the carpet.

Doorbell. Claude and the Ephraim brothers joined in, silent and understanding as co-conspirators, wasting no time on meaningless talk. The shutters were closed. Through the dark, sounds of laughter resounded. Victor proposed asking Louis to join in as well. Robby refused vehemently. He recalled his skinny, fragile friend and his sad eyes. He wanted to leave him out of it, to protect him from sin.

After they were satisfied and a bit nauseous, someone suggested going to the beach. A redeeming idea: a purifying dip; a quick one, because Claude had to get going.

"Then go," said Victor. "Who's keeping you?"

"My clothes ... they're at your house." He had borrowed a bathing suit from Robby.

Victor growled unhappily

"What are you getting angry about, like an idiot?" said Robby. "You can stay, I'll go with Claude. I'm sick of this sea anyway."

Victor looked at them suspiciously, but did not argue.

At home, while they undressed, dimples appeared in Claude's cheeks.

Robby understood and answered with a smile: Why not?

It was all done quickly, with haste. Claude was excited, knowing that his mother was already waiting for him, worried. Robby was happy to do this behind Victor's back. Claude asked Robby to come over sometime. "But without that Victor!" he said in his voice, which was too high for a boy his age.

Then Robby was left alone and sat down to draw. What should he draw? That was always the question. He never thought to draw anything he saw around him. What would he draw? He picked up drawings left behind by his two brothers who went to Israel, and began "correcting" them and giving them titles as his vandal imagination saw fit. The wonders of boredom!

If children in Alexandria were allowed at the horse races, Victor might have never taught Robby a chapter in sodomy, and his brothers' drawings might have preserved their chaste beauty.

His sister walked in and showered him with loud kisses, which she called *ventouses*, cupping. She called him *mon petit Didi*, or worse, *ma petite fille*—my little girl. Robby was never happy to hear the latter, and in his naivety sometimes even tried protesting, but whenever he did so, he was told the same story:

It was the end of December, and everyone prophesied that the baby wouldn't be born before the new year. The ninth month had gone by, and still we were waiting for a miracle.

"Why should he hurry to come out into a world of suffering?" asked Madame Marika philosophically, and shoved a piece of Turkish delight into her mouth—heaven for the tongue and hell for the teeth. Her plump face, shifting as she chewed the candy, did not seem to be in a world of suffering. But that year there was a war going on in Egypt and all over the world. The worst was behind us. After El Alamein, it was clear the war would be over in just a few months, possibly even weeks. Maybe the baby would be born into peaceful times? A new year, a year of peace … A baby, born in January, making his first steps through the world, hand in hand with the new year … Then, in the end of December, as Alexandria became a forest of Christmas trees and artificial snow fell in store windows (the only snow to be found in Egypt was that ever-prevalent cotton); as British and Australian soldiers walked the streets, drunk, singing Christmas songs and missing their faraway homes; as the sea hummed and swelled, and drops of its seething foam reached all the way to the balconies on Rue Delta—at that very moment, the contractions began. It had been eleven years since Robby's mother gave birth to Robby's sister, and she wasn't sure these were indeed contractions. Doctor Lachover was called. He whispered with her in the bedroom, and finally determined in his throaty, nasal voice, plagued by moments of falsetto (his French was tinted with an eastern European accent), "Yes, this is it. Would the lady please join me, I shall drive her to the maternity ward in my car."

"Doctor, it's going to be a girl, right?" asked Robby's eleven-year-old sister.

The doctor patted the child's head and mumbled something unclear about the mysteries of nature and God's will.

Then Grandma told the famous folktale of the rabbi who, whenever asked to foretell whether a baby would be a girl or a boy, always said, "A boy, Madame, a male child. Mazal tov!" while hiding behind the door a note that read, "Girl." If a boy was born, the rabbi humbly accepted praise; if a girl was born, as sometimes happened, the righteous rabbi would open the door with fanfare, and with a mysterious grin pick up the note and present it knowingly, saying, "I knew it was a girl ..." sigh, "but I didn't want to upset good people. I thought, maybe a miracle would happen? But I hid the truth behind this door, like a truth at the gate. What is left but to celebrate our all-knowing God?" Grandma summed up, "And what's left for us to do but to celebrate the genius rabbi?"

"I'm no genius and no rabbi," the good doctor demurred, "but even I can risk it and tell you it will be ..."

"A boy!" called Grandma.

"A girl!" cried her granddaughter.

"Forget it!" said the doctor in English, washing his

hands of prophesies.

"If it's a girl," the child vowed with her eyes closed, "*she* will be my doll. I'll toss all my dolls to the sea, or give them away to poor people."

When she heard the baby was a boy, she cried inconsolably. This is why she continued to call her brother *ma petite fille*. The grownups could do no more than to guess how his years serving as his sister's *petite fille* affected his mind and personality.

"Where have you been?" Robby asked once the tirade of kisses was over.

"Where have I been?" his sister asked with a smile. "Where everybody's been."

"At the race! Then who won?"

She smiled ironically and said, "You're dying to hear that David won, aren't you? You're dying for me to marry him, aren't you?" She shoved a finger under his arm and began tickling him.

"What's it to me?" he tried to defend himself.

"It really is nothing to you, or to anyone else in this family, but everyone's butting in, and especially your grandma!"

"Fine, don't marry him. Just tell me, who won the race?" he asked impatiently.

"Well, what do you think?"

"Going by your smile, I'd say he lost."

"You got it, genius," she said and pulled off her dress. "It's so hot today."

"He lost, huh?"

"And you know who won?"

"That Arab!" Robby said hatefully.

She danced around in her slip, gyrating her hips and waving her dress over her head.

"Stop dancing in your underwear!" Robby said angrily. "Someone might walk in. They'll all be back soon, won't they?"

"Are you worried about me, *mon cher frèrot*?" she asked and hugged him. She smelled of perfume mixed with tobacco from Ramzi's pipe. Suddenly she said, "The Arab was practically drunk with victory. His face shone with sweat, and you know what he did? He rode all the way to the English consul's loge, to pay respects to his lady, like some Ivanhoe in a knights' tournament. Then he started doing acrobatics on horseback, like a circus performer—he rode standing up, got off and on the horse while it galloped, and the crowd went mad with excitement, especially the other Arabs. Some of them even started shouting, '*Maut al yahud!* Death to the Jews!' We were a little scared, but thank God, the voices were few, just a handful of hot-headed young guys, maybe some students from the Muslim Brotherhood. They were shut down immediately. The Chief of Police, Nawas, you know him, the guy who plays *belotte* with Papa at Café Zisis, stood up and said, 'Shut your mouths, you dogs sons of dogs, or you'll get to spend a few weeks in the can!' They turned quiet right away, like good little boys. Then I saw Nawas go up to Mom, and from his gestures I could tell he was apologizing to her ..."

"What? You didn't sit with Mama and Papa?"

"No. No one knows I was at the race, and neither do you. And just you wait and see what happens if you tell anybody. We got out of there fast and Ramzi drove me home in his car."

"Ramzi!" called Robby.

"Ramzi is just a chubby guy with a heart of gold. He's crazy about me. That's all. He's no more important to me than David Hamdi-Ali, or any other guy for that matter." She hugged him to her chest and he blushed.

"So David lost. Lost," Robby lamented.

"Because I wasn't serving as his good luck charm," she said and took off her slip while walking to the bathroom. She grabbed a bathrobe on her way, and her laughter echoed through the long, dark hallway.

24. Baba au Rhum

By the time the gang arrived it was already dark. Robby's parents didn't come with them. They were invited, along with Grandma, to the house of Officer Nawas, for some coffee. The Hamdi-Alis and Murads returned to the house on Rue Delta. A silence of mourning. Joseph sat on one of the chairs in the hall and mumbled to himself, "What humiliation ... how dare he? All that wheeling and dealing ... he was putting on a show! A show! A masquerade. Shaming my son in front of everybody." This excitement did not fit the old man's general calm spirits. His small frame shrank further and he was curled up in his chair like a fetus, trembling in spite of the heavy heat. "I could kill him ... kill him ..." Suddenly he stood up and took hold of his son's shoulders. "How could you let him win, *ya ibni*? How could you let him? Didn't you think of your father?"

"What's it got to do with you?" David said, almost choking on the insolence of his own words.

"What's it got to do with me?" Joseph mumbled, and began tittering nervously, until his titters piled up to form one loud, hoarse peel of laughter.

"Joseph, you aren't feeling well!" Emilie called out with alarm.

"I feel great, Emilie. I'm as healthy as a horse. I just want to die." Then he laughed again.

David recuperated from his own words, and was ready to defend himself, but then that *jinn*, that demon, overtook him again, and he lashed out at his father once more: "I don't understand why you see it this way, *ya baba*! It isn't the end of the world. It's only sport, a race ..." And he turned his back on the man with the ecstasy of revolt.

"Sport. A race," Joseph repeated with a gloomy whisper. Then he raised his voice, "And life—is life not a game? It's because of these thoughts of yours, because of this disrespect of yours, that you lost! Because you saw it as a game, not a mission. Your enemy – he was on a mission. He was going on *jihad*. Jihad. That's why they were yelling, '*Maut al yahud!*' The entire thing has become a war of religion, a war of nations. Islam versus Judaism. They were yelling, 'Death to the Jews.' What if they decided to slaughter the Jews, what would you say then, David? Would you call that a game too? What would you say? What would you say?"

David was barely listening. He was still recovering from the shock of his own brash words, spoken to his father, and especially by the way the old man seemed to perceive them as legitimate and understandable, and accepted them without consternation, without astonishment, without violence. Suddenly David realized that a new world had opened up to him, and he was intoxicated. Through the twilight of ecstasy he heard himself speak in a different voice, a new voice: "What do you care? You're not even Jewish!"

"I ... I'm not Jewish?" the old man said meekly, pleadingly.

"I love you Mademoiselle Emilie, I love you with all my heart and soul!"—"My parents would never have it, Yusef. Never!"—"But why?"—"Because you aren't Jewish, Yusef my darling ..."

"Come on, what's the point in pretending?" David was deep in the fever of the stride, bouncing on the saddle, unable to stop. "Everybody knows you're a Muslim!" he spat, his cheeks flushed with rebellion.

"Besides, we're leaving Turkey for Alexandria!"—"I'll follow you wherever you go, my Emilie. We'll find a rabbi in Alexandria"—"A rabbi?"—"A rabbi, a rabbi to convert me and let's be done with it!"—"You're willing to... for me? Oh, Yusef, Yusef!"

"David!" cried Emilie.

Joseph chuckled to himself. So this is what it's come

to—his delicate wife has to defend him against his own son. In the past, Joseph would have beaten his son to a pulp for much smaller offenses. This time he stayed seated, almost laughing, luxuriating in his own impotence.

"Nobody would have slaughtered you, *ya baba*. You would have yelled '*Allahu akbar*' and they'd leave you be."

"This is how you treat us, Yusef my son? Your father, your mother, leaving the religion of your ancestors for a woman? Allah will punish you! Don't you fear Allah?"—"No, Papa."—"If you do so you are not my son anymore, Yusef, go. Go to your Jewish woman, and never come back ..."

"Why are you doing this to me?" Joseph mumbled in a far-off voice, as if asking with detached curiosity, as if this were an argument for the sake of argument.

"Allah will punish you!"

"Because I'm sick of it! I'm sick of dieting and being afraid. I want to eat, you hear me? I want to eat!" he screamed, and turned to the servant who rushed in at the sound of shouting. "Salem, go to the bakery and bring me half a dozen cakes!"

"Allah will punish you! Allah will punish you!"

"What kind of cakes, *ya sidi*?" Salem asked quietly and politely, as if not noticing the storm he'd just stepped into.

"Baba au rhum," spoke the ridiculing voice of Robby's sister. She appeared in a bathrobe, a towel wrapped around her head like a turban, fresh, her cheeks blushing.

"Baba au rhum, *ya sidi*?" Salem awaited David's confirmation.

"No, don't go, Salem. No! I don't want cakes. No ..." He turned to his father and dropped to his knees, put his head in the man's lap and called, "Papa, I'm sorry. I'll stick to a strict diet, I'll train and next Sunday, I'll win. I promise you, I'll win!"

"You have to, *ya ibni*. You have to win. And you will win! We'll work on it together, you and I, together, and you'll be victorious *hazben 'annu*! In spite of it all! I'm so tired." He chuckled with some vindication. "Tired." Then he got up and went to his room. His eyes reflected an exhaustion beyond words and deeds, and a sort of yearning. *You aren't Jewish*. His son said these words to him, clear as day. And what did he do? He laughed. *You aren't Jewish …*

He heard the voice of the *muezzin* from the top of the minaret, and the faithful chant curled up to him with tender trills. Yusef stood still and listened for a moment to the faraway cantillation, the words and sounds pricking his heart.

"Allah will punish you!"

He walked to his room, stooped and broken. All eyes were on him, and were then lowered once the door closed.

At that very moment, the front door opened and Victor barged in, wearing a bathing suit and sounding the battle cry of a savage.

25. Because of a Game

The yellow marble rolled on the carpet, heading toward the red marble, which was lying peacefully, unaware of its approaching fate. Crystal touched crystal—a tap. Robby jumped for joy. He's never been a good shot, which is why any hit was a victory. Victor was a lot more skilled than he was, and Robby attributed this to his friend being a year older. The marbles in their pockets collided joyously with one another.

Outside, eastern winds grunted and the sun was veiled with haze, like an eye plagued with trachoma. David and Joseph were out practicing on the tracks. Emilie tried to dissuade them from going, due to the heat wave, but her husband looked at her with contempt and dragged his son along. Ever since his loss in the match, father and son had been working ceaselessly, with fervent zealotry. David maintained a strict diet and weighed himself any chance he had. Still, he did not lose any weight. Allah's ways are wondrous and mysterious! His father was the one to lose weight. His cheeks were sunken, his hair graying, his eye sockets slowly turning black. Only the eyes burning with an alien fire hinted at the hidden treasures of raging life within this dead man's skull. "David must win!" he repeated to himself, as if possessed. As if this were a matter of life and death. He barely spoke at home. His usual taciturnity became crushing speechlessness.

Grandma sighed and said, "Did you see Emilie? She's so worried, the poor thing." She liked Emilie and was sad to see her husband treat her so badly, all for that horse racing nonsense. Had Robby's father not strictly prohibited her from interfering, she would have spoken her mind to Joseph Hamdi-Ali ages ago.

"What's that Emilie got to be so worried about?" Madame Marika said impatiently. Once more, Emilie Hamdi-Ali managed to get everyone's attention, as if the entire world revolved around her. "Big deal!"

"Wouldn't you worry, Renée, if Vita stopped eating all of a sudden?"

"Vita, stop eating? That's not a concern. He'd never give up food." She burst out in fat-jiggling laughter. "He eats and eats and never gets fat. And I fast and fast and never get thin!" Another series of loud jolts. Then she said with contempt, "People are experts in making mountains out of molehills!"

"And over horses, no less!"

"She tried to get him to go see a doctor ..."

"Did she?"

"You should have heard how he answered her. I've never heard him speak to her so rudely!" Grandma sighed.

"Those men ..." Alice said with a heavy sigh, shifting her large behind in her seat. "Each and every one of them, without exception, is bound to suddenly lash out at you with the whip of his anger, and you never know why and what for … It's so hot today … this girdle is killing me!" She looked around her, watching her friends as they formed a sort of wall of flesh to protect her from her husband Isidore's hotheadedness.

"Only my late husband was different," Aunt Tovula said unexpectedly. The other women waited on alert, not wanting to encourage her to tell yet another story they'd heard many times, and which always ended with a river of tears. But their efforts were for naught. "He never said a bad word. Never." Already she was on the brink of tears. None of the women said anything. Any talk would only serve to prolong things. Even Madame Marika held back from making a statement such as, "Your husband didn't have many chances to say anything to you, good or bad," hinting at how in his final years he lived in Jerusalem, far from his wife and children, working as a night guard at the Anglo-Palestine Bank, where he died in the great explosion on Ben Yehuda Street. Once in a while, Robby heard about his aunt taking the train to Palestine to see her husband. She'd return full of stories and experiences, but with few keepsakes and purchases, as fit her meager earnings. She stopped making the trip in 1948, because her husband was no longer alive, and the border was closed.

"My husband never said a bad word about me!"

"He must have been an angel," Madame Marika couldn't resist, but Robby's aunt was in her own world, staring out beyond her friends' ridiculing smiles. Her gaze clung to the small, green, alert eyes of her sister, Robby's grandmother. Her sister had also become a widow in the same year, 1948. Three years had gone by, the eastern winds kept blowing and their pain was slightly dulled.

The story of this unfortunate woman, who, years later, when she died in Israel, was described as not having known a moment of peace her entire life (which is a slight exaggeration), the story of this widow and her three daughters and one son, Raphael, is one of those Alexandrian stories that deserves to be told, and maybe it shall be, but our story is about the Hamdi-Alis, a family from Cairo that came to spend a summer of joy on the shores of Alex; Aunt Tovula's story must wait, along with others, for its proper time.

The conversation is back on course: "What can I tell you, good women, if you haven't heard Joseph curse in Arabic and Turkish, you haven't heard proper cursing in your life!"

"And all because Emilie dared suggest he go see a doctor?"

"As I live and breathe."

"And how did she react?"

"Locked herself in her room and cried and cried."

The women sighed. Crying, tears, that was the only outlet for women in this world of men.

"In Arabic *and* Turkish!"

A riddle floated through the air: What's going on with Joseph? His response was in no way proportionate to the scale of the catastrophe. It was clear that a much deeper crisis was taking over the old man. Something that touched his essence, his flesh, and was beyond winning or losing a race at the Alexandria Sporting Club. But who could think hard enough to figure it out in this heat and this dry air …

"Salem, *salim idak*!" Marika burst out with joy. "Bless your hands, Salem!" The servant walked in carrying a large tray with glasses of cold water and a plate of jam, snow-white and sweeter than honey, the kind Grandma called *dulce blanco*. Each woman enjoyed a spoonful of jam and a sip of refreshing water. Emilie and Joseph and the echoes of their drama melted away in all the chewing and gulping.

The only member of the Hamdi-Alis who continued with the normal course of life was Victor. No one thought of him or bothered him, everyone was preoccupied with David and his fateful race next Sunday. The marbles formed tracks through the rug. Sometimes they tapped one another, other times they overtook one another, working with a kind of secret regularity known only to them. In the dark coolness of the hall, the heat wave seemed faraway and unreal. The game went on, like a kind of ceremony, in almost complete silence. Suddenly Robby told Victor, "Your father ... why is he taking this whole thing so hard?"

Victor looked at him for a moment, as if incredulous that Robby would stop the game so abruptly only to ask such a silly question. Robby had to repeat the question before receiving an answer. "Why? Because he's stupid." Victor went back to the game and scored a nice point from a distance, while he remained standing up. He dropped Robby's marble in his pocket and waited for Robby to fulfill his part of the ritual and place another marble on the rug.

But Robby only looked at him with wonder. How could a son speak of his father this way without being struck by lightning? "How can you talk about your father that way?" he asked, appalled.

"He's stupid, I tell you." Victor saw things plainly, and did not realize that his friend still lived in a world in which parents were beyond all judgment. "He's forgetting that racing is only a game. Just like marbles. Who gets sick over a stupid game? Only fools! Put a new marble on the rug. Go on!"

Robby fished a new marble from the depths of his pocket, looked at it in a heartbreaking goodbye, and placed it down instead of the one that had been taken from him. The game went on.

Suddenly, they began shouting:

"Cheater! I saw you!"

"You saw *me*? And what exactly did I do to deserve being called a cheater?"

"You didn't toss it from your spot. You took a whole step forward, and then you scored a point. That doesn't count!"

"You don't know how to lose with dignity. You should learn from the English!"

"You and the English can kiss my ass!"

"Just say it, did I score that point or not?"

"You did, but you cheated!"

"I either scored or I didn't, that's all that matters. This marble is *mine*!"

"You won't get it, even if you stand on your head all the way to tomorrow!"

And the two wrestled on the rug, pounding each other with their fists.

They'd never fought with such rage and hatred before, and all over a silly game of marbles.

26. A Change

Two days later, the heat wave dissipated. It left as suddenly as it came, and while Alexandria savored the cool breeze, its short-term memory quickly forgot the five horrid days of heat. Once more, city-folk would argue that heat waves never hit Alexandria, that eastern winds only blow through boiling, dusty Cairo ...

Peace also overtook Joseph's face. He sat on the balcony, eyes almost closed, the wind rising from the sea caressing his square, gray mustache. He sipped his black coffee, his lips smacking with pleasure in a manner uncommon around these parts. It was clear that some sudden change had occurred in Joseph, as if all entanglements had been undone at once, and all crises evaporated as in a bad dream. At first he remained silent, but even the few sentences he spoke sounded a newfound, rather odd optimism. In all honesty, the majority of those dwelling in the apartment did not notice this change at first, and those who had did not imbue it with much significance. If it hadn't been for the events that began that day, it might have gone unnoticed. Only afterward did various wise parties begin boasting about how they foretold it all, stating, "Indeed, I could tell there was something strange about him."

Even Emilie did not see a reason to worry. Perhaps, she in particular did not. She was a natural-born optimist unable to view a positive change as an ominous sign. She was relieved and thanked God for His benevolence.

That night, in bed, she even dared snuggle up against him, feeling his body cast confidence and serenity over her, and smelling his tobacco. He caressed her softly and whispered words of love in Turkish, the language of their youth, of their intimacy, the language he spoke to Leila.

She told him how much she wanted a grandchild, and he laughed slowly.

"Why are you laughing at me, Yusef?" she asked indulgingly, choosing the eastern Turkish version of his name. It was that voice and that "Yusef" that stole his heart thirty years ago, when she was seventeen and he was thirty. That voice hadn't changed. Close your eyes and you can hear that "Yusef" being spoken by that seventeen-year-old girl, light in her eyes and music in her voice. And suddenly that girl, whose breasts had only just emerged with the force of adolescence, is talking about a grandchild, a grandchild. "Why are you laughing at me, Yusef!" she insisted, resting her head on his chest.

"I'm not laughing at you," he said quietly, almost inaudibly. They used to say about Joseph Hamdi-Ali that even when he spoke he was actually silent. Then he raised his voice and said, "I respect you and I love you. You are my *bella donna*. I left my family and my tradition and my homeland for you. You are my family, you are my tradition, you are my homeland."

Emilie accepted these words with simple joy. Pathos is at home in the East, never sparking ridicule or embarrassment in anyone but the fastidious. She accepted his words with neither pride nor guilt, as self-evident. She did not hold herself responsible for being a man's entire world and foundation. Another woman would have been filled with purpose and begun playing a role beyond her means. Emilie never thought her husband's words were intended to place some special mission upon her shoulders. Even during this crisis, her support and help came through her silence and calm, her generous expressions of love, without a word of guidance or advice. Emilie did not sense that her husband was calling to her from the depths. She did not perceive this seeming calm that had descended upon him as even more dangerous than the storms that preceded it. She didn't understand that when he said, "You are my family, you are my tradition, you are my homeland," he was merely repeating his words from the past, which were now empty, devoid of truth. Perhaps even Joseph did not know he was deceiving himself, with the fantasies he projected on the pure, white body of a seventeen-year-old. Her voice was soft and cheerful, her skin sweeter than Turkish delight. But a bird on your windowsill will sing softly and cheerfully, and yet you would not hang all of your hopes and dreams upon her … A slight tremble ran through his bones and he asked her whether the window was open.

That night, he dreamed of Leila, his horse black as night. Leila danced through the air, her open wings casting shadows on the earth, and he looked up at her and laughed and laughed— Leila was returning to him. He was still laughing when she kicked him. Even when she thrust her hooves into his stomach, he kept laughing. When she landed on his ribs, he chuckled with a moan, and when she flew back into the sky, he remained on the ground, beaten and broken. Only then did he see him, the cavalier on her back, Ahmed Kader Rahim Al-Tal'ooni.

27. I Will

"I will," read the telegram from Cairo.

Joseph smiled. He cloaked himself in silence and smiled. This was just another piece in the conspiracy forming against him, just another thread in the web that some massive spider was persistently spinning around him. Patience, he told himself with acceptance. Patience. All will be well. Like a generous host, he stood at the tent's doorway and welcomed Lilly Elhadeff with a smile.

David was embarrassed. A week and a half had passed since he sent his letter, and he'd almost forgotten the entire thing. Suddenly, not a letter in return, but a telegram! Waiting ten days to finally send a two-word telegram, no explanations included? He'd gone to the effort of writing stylized and well thought out pages. David Hamdi-Ali felt cheated. Not because she didn't respond to his letter with a simple, heartfelt one; and not because, while he piled up thousands of words, she made do with only two, two that expressed more than all of his poetics; but because at that time, he realized more clearly than ever that he did not, in fact, love Lilly Elhadeff, that her skeletal body and wooly hair left him entirely indifferent. Especially after that exciting experience in the erotic chamber of Shakra Roomy, that wizard of physical and sensual pleasures. The fact is, he did not miss her at all, though he hadn't seen her since summer started. He might not have written to her had Robby's sister not pushed him toward her with her trickery. And the most vexing thing, and perhaps the scariest, was that his heart told him that ultimately, whether he willed it or not, he would wed Lilly Elhadeff.

He remembered what she said once as they strolled on the boardwalk along the Nile in Cairo. They were almost alone, the moon was full and blue, just like in a Perrault fairy tale. A gentle wind blew among the palm trees, rustling their fronds. For a while, David sank into a pleasant nostalgia, recalling faraway legendary European medieval worlds. Castles surrounded by jagged walls, fat kings foolish and kind-hearted, queens—mostly evil, envious stepmothers—beautiful princesses donning conical hats with waving tulle, and of course *Le Prince Charmant*, who always appeared at the right moment to save his beauty from fairies or witches or dragons ... The rippling of the river and the light wind delicately caressing his face carried him to other worlds, far from the tumult of Cairo, which troubled the senses. Her delicate, cool hand was in his, calming and pleasant. He didn't look at her. In his reveries, he gave her the role of Cinderella, waiting for a miracle ...

"You see that branch?" said Lilly. Her slightly hoarse voice, often pleasant to the ear as it whispered warmly into it, now gave him chills, like chalk scratching on a blackboard. All the legends and fairies and castles evaporated into thin air.

"I see lots of branches," he answered impatiently.

"No, I mean that branch," she insisted and pointed. "You see that one?"

"Yes," he said, just to get her to shut up. If she did, he might be able to recover some of the magic. But the clock chimed midnight, the carriage stopped in its tracks and became a pumpkin once more, and not even a slipper remained on the steps. He kicked a pebble.

"Look! The palm tree is writing something in the sky," said Lilly.

"Writing?" What was she yammering about? She was always setting little traps for him, and as careful as he tried to be, he always got caught in her web. "What is it writing?" he asked with an ironic smile.

"It's writing ... hold on ... 'Da-vid ... David and ...' what? 'David and Lilly,' yes, 'David and Lilly ...' hold on, there's more: 'Ma ... David and Lilly, married!'"

"That palm tree is practically a prophet," David said, trying to sound sarcastic. "It knows things about me that even I don't know."

"It's written, David. It's written in the sky that you and I are meant to be. I didn't make it up. It says so in *le petit Livre du bon Dieu*. It also includes a date."

"Oh, yeah? And when is this blessed day?"

"We don't know. But *He* knows. Nothing we do will make any difference – you and I will be married and have children." She fixed her eyes on him, small like coffee beans. She certainly annoyed him even then, but now he was even more annoyed with himself, realizing that he, with his own hands, brought about what she called "inevitable."

Ten days of silence, and then, as if the wavering palm branch was the one writing the letter over the paper in the sky: I W I L L.

Emilie was delighted—a wedding was always a happy ending. Somebody up there heard her yearning for a grandchild. Lilly Elhadeff was a good girl, and *todo es por lo bueno*. She sighed. Why did she sigh? Who knows?

Victor hated Lilly Elhadeff the moment he first laid eyes on her. She tried to befriend him, even buying him gifts from time to time, but he only showed her his claws. She couldn't understand his animosity. Perhaps it was because she was skinny like him, and barely taller? Perhaps because she seemed like easy prey, with her frizzy hair and her small eyes? Or maybe he hated her because he thought his brother loved her? Once, she tried to caress his face, and he bit her hand. She almost passed out from the pain. David, who would normally respond to lighter offenses with a tirade of blows, burst out laughing, which added to her chagrin and humiliation.

Nevertheless, there was something seductive about Lilly. She had the same elusive magic sometimes found in puppies, or even in sick babies. Not a real, clear charm, bright and captivating, but momentary sparks of grace, and sometimes refined expressions of yet-unripe femininity, a sort of constant promise that a day will come when even Lilly Elhadeff will blossom into a woman.

28. Don't Worry, *Ya Baba*

The telegram threw David off-kilter only briefly. In the commotion of the eve of a race everything dims, even such life-altering news, especially a piece of news so bothersome that it is desirable to shove it aside. David quickly returned to his training schedule, free of unnecessary thoughts. His body was bent and coiled, the mane of his mare caressing his face, her hooves spraying gravel all over the tracks, sparks disappearing into the dust.

Joseph stood at the starting point, his pocket watch in hand. He wore only a striped shirt and a jacket. The heat was heavy and the sweat collected under his fez until it could no longer hold back, then it dripped down his face, pooling in the cracks of wrinkles. The handkerchief in his hand was soaked and smelled of something spicy and manly, somewhat intoxicating. That same sweet and familiar blurring of the senses overtook him, and within the thick ether swarming around him, he saw Leila striding in her noble loneliness, without bridle or reins, as a black fog, twisting among the vapors of dream.

"Well then, how long?"

"Well then, how long?" David repeated.

"How much time, Papa?"

David was standing next to him, breathing heavily and sweating, a thin film of dust powdering his face. "Papa!"

David shook his father's shoulder gently.

"*Ya ibni*," Joseph whispered, holding his son tightly, almost desperately.

"You worried me, *ya baba*," David said and grabbed Esperance's reins. On his way he took a sugar cube from the table and dropped it into the mare's mouth. She looked at him with kind and modest eyes.

David shook his head and rode away.

"David, *ya ibni*," his father suddenly called.

"Yes, *ya baba*," David said, turning his profile toward his father.

Joseph searched his son's face for something to lean on or hold on to, but the face was like smooth marble. There was no hint of understanding in his fair eyes. Joseph's own eyes were suddenly beholding a vision. David was going to lose the race, and not only this race. His eyes, his posture, his somewhat feminine walk, his young beauty, his simplistic fluttering, all these were taken as signs. Tal'ooni, who knew the desert like the back of his hand, he would be king of the tracks. Tal'ooni would win. Because Allah would stand at his side. Allah would not support the son of a convert. Allah would give His support to the desert rider, the image of Muhammad, His prophet.

Could a mortal change what has been written since the beginning of time? All of our actions were written the moment that Allah created the world in his wisdom, and they are written, so many scrolls, in the library of the heavens, and each day one scroll is opened, and each moment a line is read. And one of those lines says that Ahmed Al-Tal'ooni will defeat David Hamdi-Ali.

Joseph knew he had to submit to fate's decree. He could do nothing to alter that which was written in indelible ink. Now that he had gained this recognition, he was slightly relieved, but his hands were weak. He turned to leave the tracks.

Soon he heard his son call after him:

"Papa ... where to? Papa?"

"Keep training, *ya ibni*, keep going on your own," Joseph said. "I'm tired, this heat is giving me a headache."

David ran to him, grabbed his shoulders and spoke with a soothing smile: "Don't worry, *ya baba*, everything will be all right!"

Joseph shook his head as if to say, you are kind for encouraging your father, but I do not believe it. He walked on.

David remained alone on the tracks. He watched his father walking away, bent over, and pitied him for being so old and tired. The sight of his father wilting in the afternoon sun paradoxically encouraged him, and he experienced a wave of energy. The father bequeaths to his son his fame and fortune, his entire being and then climbs up a dry mountain, his head disappearing among the white clouds of old age and decrepitude. He once read about such a custom among primitive tribes. At the time, he thought it was cruel and barbaric. Now watching his father's decline, it seemed almost natural. With gallant speed he hopped on his mare, hugged her neck and sank his head into her mane. The pungent smell of the beast sent stunning, intoxicating waves through him. He kicked his heels into her stomach and urged her to gallop onto the tracks, to the protests of the Arab groom who stayed behind, saddle and reins in hand.

How much confidence and strength he drew from riding bareback, this sensual clinging to the mare's hot, sweaty neck, as if something of her strong, flexible muscles seeped into his own body. She galloped fast and wild, but all the while careful not to throw off her master who clung to her with addiction, yet also with a measure of fear. Any moment he could slip and fall. The groom called after him that it was irresponsible madness, taking such a risk two days before the race. He threatened the *sidi* that he would tell his father, but David didn't care. He was happy, breathlessly happy, and did not know why. He was free, the wind mussing his blond hair, chasing him and Esperance, unable to catch them.

If only Robby's sister could see him now.

29. IN THE ACT

Robby could not understand, after the fact, how he and Victor could have been so lax as to let his mother catch them in the act.

He was sure his mother would take extraordinary measures and give him an honest beating, and worse yet, run to tell all the tenants what she'd seen. The shame! He stood before her, eyes downcast, his heart filled with that retrospective question—what was this even good for? The pleasure was not worth this humiliation, standing there against his mother's reproachful eyes. Victor stood there too, his underwear hanging loose over his body, and tauntingly watched Robby's mother, as if saying, It's clear you're even more embarrassed than we are, and you don't know what to do. You must wish you'd pretended not to see a thing.

"Do you know, Robby, that you can catch diseases like that?" she finally said, ignoring Victor completely. Robby's stomach turned inside him. She knew, perhaps in wisdom rather than cunning, how to cater to his weakness and his hypochondria. Was this merely a trick meant to scare him off, or did she truly believe that these naive acts of sodomy could cause intestinal or venereal diseases or God knows what? We all knew that homosexual intercourse was against nature, correct? It was unacceptable in a decent society, n'est-ce-pas? Perhaps the Arabs, among themselves, who knows ... She was truly shocked. She must have wondered where they learned such things. It must have been Victor, that miscreant, who taught my little Robbico ... She sighed and continued, "Terrible diseases!" She did not elaborate, and Robby preferred not to ask. At best, this was some sort of gut-twisting dysentery. The mere thought scared him so much that he felt lava churning in his stomach, and cold sweat covered his forehead.

"If you promise never to do it again, I'll promise not to tell your father," she said, ignoring Victor once more.

Robby quickly promised and swore silently to keep his word. In his imagination, he pictured himself standing before his father's steel gaze, a combination of contempt and disappointment. The image was too much for him to bear. He was grateful to his mother for saving him from this, for it was easier for her to handle it discreetly. Robby was a responsible child, and he decided to be worthy of this special treatment. He hated Victor Hamdi-Ali for dragging him into this mess in the first place, and left the room with his mother without giving him so much as another look. Victor stayed put, pulling up his loose underwear. His attitude was practical: if the lady told only his mother, he'd be scot-free. If she should choose to tell his father, or worse yet, his brother ... but he quickly waved off these possibilities. He knew women were more comfortable settling such delicate matters among themselves. Of course, Emilie Hamdi-Ali could also decide to share this matter with her husband or her eldest son ... but Victor viewed this option as highly unlikely. His merciful mother would be so scared of their harsh reactions that she would prefer to handle this matter on her own. And he would work things out with her somehow. When he weighed the matter further he became certain that his mother would be too embarrassed to even acknowledge the problem at all; she would turn a blind eye and pretend to know nothing. Encouraged by this series of conclusions, he grabbed his fishing rod and went out to the hall. Robby was already wearing his pants again. Victor didn't even invite him to the beach. He only smiled condescendingly. Robby gritted his teeth and said nothing.

30. Arabesque

When Joseph Hamdi-Ali returned from the tracks that day, he lay on his bed and refused to drink coffee. Exhaustion filled his body, as if some chilly serum had dripped and become absorbed into his marrow. He welcomed the illness, or at least accepted it with a fatalistic greeting. There's something about being ill that liberates you from all trivial obligations. Suddenly it is the focal point, pushing away other hardships. The sick man becomes familiar with his body and intimate with his soul, knowing that on that final long journey he will not be joined by wife, children or doctors. What would he say when he'd come face-to-face with his maker? Years ago, he turned his back on the religion of his fathers, following his heart, his whims … Is it Allah sitting up there in the heavens, upon a high throne, floating in the Nile of paradise, or is it the God of the Jews? It's not to be excluded that they're one and the same God, just as Abraham was the father of both Isaac and Ishmael, one father for us all, one God, each man seeing Him through his own eyes, one with the eyes of a Jew, another with the eyes of a Christian, another yet with the eyes of a Muslim. Then one man would say to another, "You see? I was right, God is Jewish!" And the other would say, "No, I was right! God is Christian, can't you see His halo?" "That's a skullcap, you're blind!" the Jew would call out, laughing. Then the Muslim would stand up and declare, "Neither a halo nor a skullcap. What you see is the headband that holds his *kaffiyeh* in place." And the three would go on arguing through eternity. Joseph laughed bitterly— there is no certainty, even up there! Even up there we are deceived by our senses; even up there, those damned wars of faith carry on. Impatiently, he pushed away the bothersome thought and saw that same patriarch, that wondrous father of all peoples, smiling at him and saying pleasantly, Yusef, you are my son, and whether you call me Allah or Jehova, or even *le bon Dieu*, I am one in Heaven and on earth, and there is no other but Me. I've had many prophets. Just like this delta, which is one river splitting into many arms. Each arm says, Only I belong to my father, the river. But the birds in the sky know that the river has many children, and that these tributaries are but one. The truth has many faces, but it is only one truth …

Yusef Hamdi-Ali's father was a clerk at the courthouse in Izmir. He made his living writing letters of appeal to the court for the illiterate. Sometimes he wrote love letters for them in decorative handwriting. Sometimes he would amuse himself by embellishing people's letters with complex and ravishing arabesques. Yusef remembered the legendary creatures his father would conjure up so easily on yellowing paper. In his few free hours he would read and interpret to his son the mysterious contents of these compositions, which contained the essence and life of Islam.

Why was he remembering these calligraphic acrobatics of the virtuoso scribe now, of all times? For a moment he dozed off and saw himself trapped in the curlicues of one such arabesque, trying to free himself of the thicket of letters.

The dream was short, a blink of an eye, perhaps no time at all, perhaps eternity. Outside the window, an unreal sky winked at him. Joseph's eyes were wide open, and a serenity he'd never experienced before descended upon him.

Leila strode slowly and sensually among fields and clouds, and Yusef settled on her bare back and was carried away on the wings of a dream.

31. In a Foreign Land

Once, long ago when Joseph Hamdi-Ali was young and Leila enjoyed fame, the jockey and his mare were invited to race against the best jockeys and horses in Europe, at the Royal Ascot race in Berkshire, England. King George himself was to grace the event held each June with his royal presence. All of Britain prayed for mild weather, for in this faraway, northern land, it rained even in summer.

During the ten-day journey by ship to the British Isles, Leila was already restless. Joseph hired a special veterinarian to escort them. Those days, Joseph was rich and famous, and though he was never handsome, he had a seductive Eastern allure. Many women were prepared to join him in bed, especially on those long days of sea and sky. But he turned them all down with glum zealotry and remained faithful to his Emilie, and to his Leila. The veterinarian saw nothing out of the ordinary and reassured Joseph, jokingly telling him that a mare taken from her habitat would have a natural tendency toward depression, just as can occur in the best human families, and that Joseph had nothing to worry about.

Some time later, Joseph recalled those days of bright sun and flickering water, those days spent deep in the darkness of Leila's special cabin, wondering what made her spirits so low and what was preventing her from eating. When he remembered all this, he knew for certain that Leila already foresaw what was in store for her in that foreign land of heavy clouds, and was sending him a silent warning, but he took no notice, purposely ignoring her desperate cry for help. He would not give up the promise of fame and fortune.

He, Joseph, left his homeland in his youth, turning his back on tradition, and went in search of greener pastures. He wandered across land and sea, never feeling that dull pain at the spot where his roots were torn from the ground.

But his mare did. Quick, easy, vulgar adaptation is not the way of nobility. Several years earlier, when she was uprooted from the great desert landscape and trapped among the fences of the giant tracks at the Gezira Sporting Club in Cairo, it took her weeks and months before she agreed to make do with an enclosed space, even though the tracks were so big that from certain angles the fence was nowhere to be seen. Joseph knew that when Leila felt stifled she stared longingly at the horizon of yellow desert dunes, encompassing endless space. At first Leila was rebellious and melancholic, and indifferent at best. Joseph was desperate. He'd spent his savings on her, hoping to rebuild a fortune off her, and had been bitterly disappointed. He often asked himself why he'd been tempted to purchase her at all. He even entertained the thought of selling her, despite the financial loss. But then, one bright morning, without any warning, she grew wings and spread them with nobility and grace, and overwhelming power.

Now Joseph sat at her side in the gloomy cabin of the ship and told himself, She'll pull through … she'll pull through …

The weather in Ascot was gray and dreary. Tiny drops of rain floated like dust through the heavy, hot air. Jockey and mare were somber, their heads hanging low. Yusef didn't cheer up even when his promised payment was received. He and his mare were exiles. On the decisive day the grassy tracks were slippery and treacherous. Joseph expected the race to be cancelled or postponed due to the weather, but when black umbrellas began popping up like mushrooms, he realized that Europeans did not change their plans due to a drizzle. The race would be held as planned.

Did she slip on the muddy ground, losing her footing? Did she trip, taking an incautious step?

Everyone knows what happened next. Leila died in

that foreign, unforgiving land. Leila died and the rain fell harder and harder and the ladies and gentlemen of Ascot fled from the storm. Leila was dead and no shipping company agreed to transport the carcass of a mare all the way to Egypt. Joseph was forced to leave Leila behind, and return to Alexandria alone.

This happened long ago, and one might assume it had been forgotten. After all, she was only a mare.

The illness lasted three days and three nights.

32. EYEWITNESS

His leaving the house suddenly on the morning of the race made everyone suspicious and restless. Why did Joseph Hamdi-Ali choose to leave the house that morning, of all times? For three days he had laid in bed as if in another world, cavorting with angels, as if everyday matters were beyond him, the smile of death hovering over his face, and now suddenly he'd jumped out of bed, put on a clean, ironed shirt, a short jacket, his fez, and left with haste. Not just for a stroll, people would say after the fact. It was the exit of a determined man.

"He was seen walking into the pharmacy on the corner," Madame Marika would say decisively.

General protest: Seen by whom? God save us from gossip! *Que Dieu nous protège des mauvaises langues!*

"I heard it from my Vita," Madame Marika said to absolve herself of responsibility for her accusatory statement.

"And who did your Vita hear it from?" several voices asked at once. Some believed and wanted to know how Vita found out, certain that neither Vita nor Renée Marika invented the story. Others saw the entire tale as irresponsible slander, and asked the question ironically. They weren't expecting an answer, but rather a shrug.

But a woman like Marika was not one to give in to pressure. She quickly quipped, "From his sister, from Victoria herself."

"And Victoria—where from?"

"Yes, Victoria, who did she hear it from?"

"Did *she* see Joseph?"

"Was she what you'd call an eyewitness?"

"Or did she hear it from someone else as well?"

"Why don't you go and ask her yourselves!"

Someone made the effort to go to the Sporting neighborhood and ask Victoria herself. It turned out that her servant, Gamila, had seen a short, skinny man in a fez walking into the pharmacy.

"And is Joseph Hamdi-Ali the only short, skinny man who wears a fez in all of Alexandria?"

They interrogated the boy who worked at the pharmacy, a bespectacled Syrian whose French was *vraiment impeccable*. He answered the female contingent with perfect manners, but they couldn't glean much from his words. In his generosity and graciousness he might have even tried to agree with those who claimed that Joseph wasn't at the pharmacy that morning, as well as with those who claimed he was. Upon leaving, the ladies could agree only on one thing – the man was certainly *charmant*, but none of them could say he gave a clear answer.

No one knew anything. We asked our late grandmother, when she was still alive, and she couldn't answer such a seemingly simple question either: Did Joseph Hamdi-Ali visit the pharmacy that summer's day? And if so, did he buy a toothbrush or some brilliantine for his hair, or perhaps something else … something which was later presented in court as Exhibit A?

Grandma told us there were people who tried to jump to conclusions and judge Joseph Hamdi-Ali by the way his life ended, and who said that what he did afterward proved it all: Had he not known he was guilty, why would he have acted the way he had?

Grandma disputed this view. Grandma, illiterate but shrewd, disputed this by asking a simple question: Since when is everything we do a result of our previous actions? She didn't ask it quite this way, of course, having spoken Ladino, a language in which things sound differently. At any rate, no matter how we look at it, we find ourselves returning once more to Leila, striding calmly among the clouds, wavy and graceful as silk, almost feline, eternal.

33. STAIN

His deterioration began after Leila's death. Joseph would not replace her. Cards and raki, and perhaps other women, who knows? Emilie certainly didn't know. He'd disappear for entire days, sometimes nights too, and when he'd return, worn out and ragged, nerves shot, Emilie would welcome him as if nothing happened, as if everything was as it always had been. She cooked him food which he barely touched. She tried to make love to him, usually unsuccessfully. She told him of the child's accomplishments at school. She didn't tell him that their money, not only the large fortune he'd accumulated in his years as a jockey, but even the insurance money they'd received upon Leila's death, was running out. Some say Victor was conceived on one of those tortured nights, and that this is the cause of his strangeness. Who knows?

One fine morning, when David was seventeen, his father came to school, pulled him out of class, ignoring the teacher's protests, and took him away. He bought him a mare and paid with a check, not knowing it would bounce. When Emilie found out she ran to her father and groveled at his feet, threatening to kill herself. The shocked old man pulled out his wallet. Joseph began training his son in riding the new mare, called Esperance, for she represented hope. David learned quickly. He'd inherited his father's agility on horseback, though he clearly lacked that passionate devotion on the tracks. It didn't take long before the Hamdi-Ali team began making waves. Money slowly began flowing back to the family. Emilie returned her father's loan and never told her husband a thing. She smiled happily: God hadn't let her down. Now everything would be as it once was, before Leila had died. She was sure Esperance would take Leila's place. The bad years were over. Maybe one or two white hairs. A five-year-old child clinging to her leg. She had a special affection for that boy, or perhaps it was pity. His heart-wrenching ugliness, the strangeness of his manners. But he was only a baby. When he grew up things would work out, Emilie told herself, though deep inside she resigned herself to a different fate for him. It was clear he would never be like David. And so what? Did all children have to be like David? She watched her eldest son with pride as he leaned into the mare's back, a reflection blurred by dust and speed. She would sit in the loge wearing a small brimmed hat, ruffles cascading against her eyes. She followed her son through small binoculars. A seventeen-year-old boy, and that giant horse obeyed him as if he were God. One day they'd be rich again thanks to that boy. Joseph expected it to happen within three, or maybe four years ...

Three years, four years, five—she wasn't getting any younger, but she had no complaints. Once more he sat there bent over the horse, and it was clear he would win. Emilie had no doubt about it. She brought the binoculars to her eyes.

The horses stood in a row, every muscle flexed and prepared. The jockeys bent over them, their visors turned back. Any unnecessary protrusion could set them back. A horse and a jockey must be one aerodynamic unit, like a bullet shot from a gun. The row of horses at the starting line is long, the competition great, but all minds and hearts are set on only two contestants. They all know only two are battling today. A tournament of two.

Al-Tal'ooni's black eyes looked ahead stubbornly. Emilie's binoculars fixed on her son's bright blue eyes, which wandered around with bored indifference. They all awaited the signal. Flies swarmed around the moist corners of the patient horses' eyes. One might wonder what makes them run, these slender beasts? They know nothing of the bets placed and pending in the hot, stifling air of an Alexandrian summer's day. Is it an innate sense of competition that shoots adrenaline into their hooves? They cannot be moved by external forces only, by the spurs in their sides and the reins around their necks. Perhaps it's the brotherhood of man and beast? Or maybe this love, this sensual love that turns the wheels of the world, which also animates this graceful, magical gallop, making your breath speed and your throat let out cries of excitement you'd never dare sound in a respectable salon, sitting down to a game of cards.

Al-Tal'ooni must have been certain that the bond between him and his horse was the main factor in his success on the track. They said that Ahmed had never loved a woman. Even if the rumors about him and the consul's wife were true, it clearly wasn't love. They said he never loved his mother and his father, and that he despised his many brothers. He loved the desert, but even that love he abandoned for greener pastures. The track was a small-scale desert for him. Occasionally he disappeared from the city, riding out to the dunes. He'd often been seen on the beaches of Lake Mariout, riding around, his white gown blowing in the breeze. Some said he did it for the newspapers, as a form of public relations, creating the image of a legendary hero from *Arabian Nights*, his life filled with mystery and fantasy. Leila loved the desert too, Joseph thought to himself and shook his head, as if trying to push away a disturbing thought. Ahmed and his horse, Al Buraq, named for the mythical steed that transported the prophet Muhammad from Mecca to Jerusalem, were like one being, perfection; no one could tell where the man ended and the horse began. That's just the kind of thing people used to say about him and Leila. Is it any wonder, then, that the day Leila left him, flying off to gallop in the eternal fields of heaven, Joseph retired from the track and never rode again?

Not David. He did not see the mystical, romantic side of things. He loved Esperance and could have said (and if he didn't dare, we would say it for him) that in his affinity toward her he sometimes experienced emotions and exultation close to that felt with a beloved woman. But this cult of the animal was nowhere near a bond of love, *mon vieux*! Joseph turned to horse racing because his soul could find peace nowhere but on the track. David turned to horse racing because his father had been in the trade before him, and because he admired his jockey father as a child, and because he was promised he could get rich.

In the past—when was it?—Joseph had some dim hopes for his son as his true successor on the track, the one who would seamlessly continue the career he'd started. Now as Joseph waited breathlessly for the signal, he had no illusions. Even if his son won the race, it was all a lie. A deception, trickery. Joseph might have even looked forward to his son's defeat, or at least accepted it. His son did not deserve to win this race, and since it was all predetermined, and nothing was incidental, there was no reason to assume that the unworthy one would win, even if he was Joseph Hamdi-Ali's son. For a moment, he felt a strange closeness to the dark Arab, who looked slightly ridiculous in his colorful jockey's outfit and funny cap, so European, looking as if the cap just happened to fall on his head. But of course, this was only when he stood waiting with the other riders. Not when he flew upon the wind, clouds of dust swirling around him. In those moments he resembled a *simoom*, an eastern desert storm that blew in and altered the face of the desert in an instant.

Joseph Hamdi-Ali closed his eyes. Some say they remained closed for the whole race, a fact which gave rise to contradictory interpretations. Some saw it as an incriminating sign, others as a virtue. Some argued that he closed his eyes from fear and guilt, while others claimed that had he really done something foolish and unworthy, he would not have been able to help himself from following the events with open eyes to make sure that his scheme bore fruit.

When he opened his eyes, David had already won. The boy was peacocking away, all smiles and pride. His victory was complete.

Complete? Some questioned this.

General confusion led to doubt. The truth was, and almost everyone admitted it, in the middle of the race Al Buraq began acting out of character, strangely, as if he had no intention of reaching the finish line first. Ahmed tried with all his might to control the dazed beast, but when he finally managed to, only a few seconds later, it was already too late. And in spite of this delay, he still came in second. Second! How much contempt is contained in this word! The difference between second and first is the same as the difference between relative and absolute. This fact was etched on the slate of eternity: Esperance came in a head before Al Buraq. A head might as well be an abyss. Desperation and rage rose, swelled, bubbled as if from the depths of a volcano. Something had to be done, right away! Something had to be done, somehow he had to turn back the hands of time. What was wrong with Al Buraq? Did he suddenly fall ill? And if he did, was it spontaneous or … or … it can't be! But why not? That had to be it. And even if it wasn't, this was the moment to cry out in protest. A moment longer, and it would be too late.

A hair-raising cry of grief left the wrathful Bedouin's mouth, and though it stank of bad acting, it still managed to shake up the crowd. Some people revolted against the vulgar act, saw it as losing without dignity. But the majority heard entirely different echoes in this cry. Awhile later, in court, some claimed they heard in that cry the protest of all Egypt, trampled under the feet of strangers. Baseless statements, indeed, and yet they might explain the wave of national chaos that began at the racetrack and submerged the entire beachfront of Alexandria. But let us not get ahead of ourselves.

Ahmed Al-Tal'ooni knew that in spite of the impression made by his theatricalities, the echoes would soon die down if he didn't make an explicit statement. Now it was time to point an accusing finger. A ridiculous scheme. Nevertheless …

"Someone drugged my Al Buraq!"

After the initial shock, there came a mélange of calls of agreement and calls of derision and scorn. First the louder voices were those rejecting such a capricious, unfounded accusation. It was an easy out, an act of childishness, they said. Anyone losing a competition could claim foul play and ask for a recall. But rationality has nothing to do with reality. Against these voices, a dark, consolidated call formulated, sounding agreement in primitive beats, growing louder until they became a threatening thunder, closing in tight, stifling circles, desperately trying to break through.

Someone sensed the nearing danger and called out to the fallen knight: "Who? Please, tell us, who did this terrible thing?"

Who?

The question echoed in Al-Tal'ooni's mind. So far he hadn't given it much thought. Now he had to answer fast, before the impression was dulled. Should he blame his Jewish rival himself? He was about to shout hysterically,

Daoud Hamdi-Ali, he's the one who drugged my horse! But at that moment his gaze fell upon two sharp eyes.

Al-Tal'ooni's embarrassment only lasted a moment.

Maybe Ahmed saw guilt flickering in the old man's eyes, or perhaps he saw the reflection of his own slander, or perhaps he merely saw a suitable victim to latch on to. One thing was clear—Al-Tal'ooni's cry, "That old man ... that damned old man ... he's the one who drugged my horse ... Allah, avenge me, avenge me, Allah! I have ... I have proof that he ... he ... it was him!"

Joseph Hamdi-Ali heard these things and yet did not hear them. Or perhaps he heard them but they simply didn't register. People crowded around him. Some of his friends pressed him to respond immediately and harshly to this evil slander. Joseph Hamdi-Ali only smiled his usual smile. That hospitable smile known only to sons of the Levant, that smile of acceptance which welcomes calamity. He shook his head and closed his eyes. He was in his own world. That light anxiety, watered down with awkward glee, which gripped him when he learned of his son's victory, now gave way to fatalistic serenity. He knew now: his son's victory was a ruse, granting him a short, deceitful moment of illusion, only to inflict upon him, him and not his son, a blow far worse than any he could previously imagine—slander. This petty betrayal by Al-Tal'ooni. How contemptible, how insulting, for his good name and his professional integrity to be manipulated like toys, passed from hand to hand, each handler staining them further.

And now, with precious moments passing, and Al-Tal'ooni prancing about in an hysterical display, and Joeph Hamdi-Ali seemingly sinking deeper into his own defeat ... Suddenly the old Turk pounced with out-stretched arms at the young Arab's throat.

Luckily, the two were pulled apart. Officer Nawas, Robby's father's good friend, arrived within seconds, and a phalanx of police officers came between the foes. They managed, for the time being, to scare away the Arab mob wildly supporting their hero, whose throat emitted gurgling sounds from the steel grip of the Jew's fingers.

"*Maut al yahud!* Death to the Jews!" the calls came.

"*Sahyuni! Sahyuni!*" others shouted. "Zionist!"—that classic opening for riots and protests, for unloading deep, bitter disappointment.

Nawas and his colleagues tried to stem the tide by shouting back curses of their own. "*Klab ibn'l klab,*" they shouted, "Dogs sons of dogs," and brandished their wooden clubs. But they were too few, and the crowd's rage rose with each passing moment. Later on, after the Officers' Revolution led by Muhammad Naguib and Gamal Abdel Nasser, it was discovered that on that day all sorts of factors incited the crowd, factors with different and even contradicting interests, nevertheless united in their hatred of any overprivileged stranger, and first and foremost, of the British administration. There were representatives of the Muslim Brotherhood, fanatical and violent, and then there were a handful of left-wing students with socialist inclinations, those who within the year would become the most enthusiastic supporters of the Free Officers Movement. Any reason was good enough for an anti-British and anti-Zionist demonstration, for a spontaneous expression of the resentment felt by Egyptians, who saw themselves as having been cheated for centuries.

Nawas managed to sneak the Hamdi-Alis out of the track, but the mob was now on the streets, unloading its anguish in a sort of carnival that comprised more noise than actual violence. Nevertheless, these protests melted even the bravest hearts, and certainly Grandma's heart, which had never been too brave. As the protest spilled into the streets, she was on the tram with her friend Renée Marika, on their way home from a visit to Grandma's sister, Robby's rich great-aunt, who lived in a luxury apartment in the Cleopatra neighborhood. That day they hadn't gone to the race, since Robby's parents hadn't either. The Ford offices in Alexandria, where Robby's father worked, were about to relocate to a modern, expanded complex in Smooha neighborhood, and on that stifling Sunday, employees and their families were invited to a reception to inaugurate the facilities. Robby was there too, proud and happy when his father showed him his new office. Shortly thereafter, his father quit his job as a result of conflict with his supervisor, a Brit with clear anti-Semitic tendencies. In the winter of 1951, the family left the shores of Alexandria by boat, perhaps forever.

For some reason, the protestors chose to march along the tram tracks, disrupting traffic. Robby's grandmother and Madam Marika's tram was also halted, and several protestors got on, like robbers on postal trains in the Wild West, shouting slogans and ambiguous threats. One of them stopped by the two ladies, looked at them carefully as their breath caught in their chests, and muttered in an ominous tone, "*Yahudi?*"

Robby's grandmother, by her own account, almost wet her pants with fear. She was speechless. Her face attested louder than a hundred witnesses to her Jewish identity, and, as a result, to her friend's as well. They were left to pray to the heavens, and they might really have needed a miracle, if not for Renée Marika's resourcefulness. That very moment she smiled mischievously. "Us? Of course not. We're Greek, are we not, Kiria Papadopulos?" she said, turning to her pale friend.

"*Né, né*," answered Grandma in the language of Homer. "Yes, yes." Then the two went on to converse freely in Greek, until the man shrugged and moved to another car. They continued conversing *en grégo* even after getting off the train. The two had been fluent in the language ever since their childhoods spent in Balkan territories with shifting borders. Robby's grandmother was from the town of Dedeagach by the Dardanelles, an area with much experience in the Greco-Turkish War, and later named Alexandroupoli. Renée Marika was born in Rhodes. Greek was her mother tongue, along with Ladino—which we used to call *Español*—the language of nostalgia, each word giving way to yearning for faraway Spain, with which we've had such a tumultuous romance.

That evening the protests died down, and by the time Robby got home no trace was left of them. The protestors did not smash store windows or set tires on fire. True, they screamed at the tops of their lungs, but such screams dissipate in the twilight, when a light breeze blows, allowing throats to breathe freely, fear to diminish and the heart to rejoice.

34. INVESTIGATING JUDGE

The investigating judge flipped through the dossier disinterestedly. Hamdi-Ali, Tal'ooni. Suddenly his curiosity was piqued, realizing that Hamdi-Ali was Jewish, in spite of his seemingly Arab name. The investigating judge had no issue with Jews. Many of his friends were Jewish, and he was proud of that. Tal'ooni v. Hamdi-Ali. He didn't like mixed cases, where animosity between nationalities and religions complicated a conflict between two men. Well, what have we got here? Drugging a horse in an attempt to fix a race and ... attempted murder. Attempted murder? Well ...

The heat in the dark office was unbearable. An exhausted ceiling fan lazily dragged its blades, its hum putting the investigating judge to sleep. A fly circled his nose. "George!" he called to his Coptic assistant, sitting in the adjacent office in front of piles of paperwork. George returned his pen to its blotter and ran in bowing to hear his supervisor's wishes.

"*Ahwa*," said the lawman, swallowing the first letter of the word for coffee, *qahwa*. In Egypt no one pronounced that heavy *q*, which might be why Egyptian Arabic always sounded more refined to the European ear.

"*Aywa, ya sidi*," answered the young clerk, pushing his fez slightly in subordination.

Maybe the coffee would wake him up, the investigating judge thought, and shot George an affectionate, paternal smile. With deep gratitude, the young man bowed his way back out the door. Accompanied by a symphony of typewriters, he walked down the depressing gray hallway. When he reached the young secretary at the end of the passage he saw her putting on makeup in front of a small compact mirror. She spotted him from the corner of her eye and quickly hid her makeup kit, but she'd been caught. George said nothing. His accusing look was more than enough. "The old man wants a coffee," he said with authority. His mission had been accomplished and he returned to drown in paperwork.

The girl stood up, walked downstairs to the doorman and gave him the order. The doorman looked aggravated, but jumped up immediately. "Khaled! *Ya bne'l kalb*, you son of a bitch, wake up!" he called out. Khaled, his young son, would be the one to walk the two hundred yards to the nearest café. "*Sukar ziada!*" Extra sugar, the doorman ordered. "It's for the bey," he added with importance. The bey liked his coffee sweet. To tell the truth, the investigating judge wasn't really a "bey" at all, but he enjoyed the doorman addressing him as such, and sometimes repaid him with bakshish. Out of sincere gratitude, the doorman continued to use the title even when the judge wasn't around, and especially when speaking to his son, Khaled. He wanted to make sure the title became engrained in him as well, so he never forgot to use it when in the presence of the great man.

The coffee was brought over by the café owner himself,

in peasant pants, a hooked mustache and a jaunty fez. He wouldn't take the risk of entrusting the high clerk's coffee to the hands of one of his employees, who, with their pigheadedness, might lose the kaimak. Then the bey might complain that the coffee he sells is nothing but sewer water. Once the coffee was placed in front of the investigating judge, along with a glass of very cold water, the man sighed deeply and said nothing. The café owner immediately asked the reason for this heavy sigh.

"When your father, God have mercy on his soul, ran the café, he always brought along a little *shisha*, without me having to ask ..." He sighed again and added philosophically, "The things we receive without having to ask, those are the things that bring us real pleasure." And he sighed once more, as if to say, Nobody bothers to uphold standards anymore ...

"I'll send the boy over right away with —"

The clerk fixed his eyes on him, and the café owner hurried to correct himself. "I'll bring one over myself."

The clerk smiled and tossed a coin his way.

The coffee and the shisha and the cold water alleviated the judge's sweaty and sticky summer malaise. Even the limp fan seemed to have regained some of its youthful energy.

Al-Tal'ooni v. Hamdi-Ali.

The horse racing business.

The judge, who was addicted to cards and dice, could not understand why people got so worked up about horse racing.

"'Attempted murder.' *Esh da?* What does that mean?"

He read through the investigation report and the charge sheet. He wrote with pencil in the margins, "assault" instead of "attempted murder." An old man, nearing seventy, against a young man of twenty-five-years. He shook his head. People had nothing better to do these days. The protests worried him quite a bit as well.

The police had arrested some of the loudest big-mouths of the mob, but deep inside he knew that something was cooking in the outskirts, something was bubbling beneath the surface. I can feel it in the soles of my feet, he thought, and when it erupts, no one will be safe. Not even His Majesty, the King. Especially not the king. He set his eyes on the portrait of the young, auspicious Prince Farouk, handsome, smiling Farouk, the way he looked on that hopeful day when he disembarked from the ship that returned him from England to Egypt upon the death of his father, King Fouad. Now Farouk was fat and corrupt. Will they use a guillotine, like in France? A gun in the basement, à *la russe*? And he, a rather lowly investigating judge—will he be considered small fry, someone not worthy of consideration, or will he earn the honor of being named Enemy of the People, a term so favored by revolutionaries the world over? Why can't things just remain as they were?

George walked in to announce the arrival of the litigants with their attorneys. The investigating judge finished the remains of his coffee, put the shisha aside, grabbed his prayer beads and sat down ceremoniously behind his heavy black desk.

The litigants and their representatives walked in and seated themselves on the benches across from one another. The fly landed on Al-Tal'ooni's nose. He smashed it with a single blow. The investigating judge was put off by such cruelty and impatience, but deep inside he was impressed. That fly had been pestering him since morning and he'd done nothing about it, and now this young man comes in from the desert like a bolt of lightning.

It wasn't easy to persuade the stubborn Bedouin to change the indictment. He insisted on "attempted murder" and claimed he'd barely escaped the old man's claws. Al-Tal'ooni's attorney agreed with the investigating judge that the accusation was exaggerated, and added that it hurt their chances of conviction.

35. *No Es A La Moda Hoy*

Joseph sat low on the bench, separate and solitary. He'd heard the words spoken around him only dimly: What difference did it make, he thought, if it was assault or attempted murder? He didn't care about the legal implications. He was much more upset about the other accusation, the allegedly lesser one, that he'd tried to drug the horse. Any dignified man might lose his mind once and try to strangle his opponent. It's natural, it's human, there's no disgrace in that. But drugging a horse—that is a pathetic act of fraud which tarnishes the name of the perpetrator. Whenever anyone mentioned the matter in passing, Joseph felt a pang in his heart.

Should we infer from this that Joseph was innocent? That he was not the one to inject the horse with an anesthetizing, paralyzing drug? A blood test performed on the horse found a considerable amount of some such substance. That's why Al Buraq had not performed according to his natural abilities, and since he lost only by a head, people were sure he would have won if not for this fact. But can we conclude from this that Joseph Hamdi-Ali was the one to do the deed? And if not him –who? Maybe his son David? But that would be almost the same. And if we begin guessing, we might even argue that Tal'ooni himself, or better yet, his trainer, that conniving Greek, fearing they might lose the race, and in order to sabotage their opponent, were the ones doing the drugging. True, this conjecture was overreaching, but no more absurd than some of the others voiced.

At any rate, Joseph denied the allegations fervently. He calmly described his years of working at the track and his irreproachable past. When asked whether he in fact tried to murder Al-Tal'ooni, he said, "I'm sorry they pulled us apart!"

His attorney complained to Joseph's wife and son that Monsieur Hamdi-Ali wasn't cooperating and wasn't helping himself. "*Il est excessivement honnête!*" he said, shaking his head. He's being too honest!

"*No es a la moda hoy de ser tanto honesto.*" Meaning, it isn't fashionable to be too honest these days. That was grandmother's opinion on the matter, expressed to her card-playing friends. Renée Marika agreed wholeheartedly, "Only fools are too honest. Take my Vita for example ..." She began ranting about her husband Vita's legendary integrity, her voice full of both admiration and ridicule, the way we discuss prophets or heroes. Then Aunt Tovula called out, "So is my Moïse," and began describing the lofty character of her late husband, her words saturated with yearning and pain. But she didn't get a chance to finish either. Robby's grandmother chimed in, praising the vaunted sincerity of her husband, may he rest in peace, until she finally returned to her thesis on how it is unfashionable to be too honest these days.

36. Tears

Panayotti was shocked and agitated, pacing the room. "How could I, Joseph, *mon ami, ya habibi*, how? Have you thought about what you're asking me?"

"I didn't have much faith in you anyway," Joseph said drily and got up to leave. He paused for a moment to look at the large photo on Panayotti's office wall—Al-Tal'ooni atop Al Buraq, the horse rearing high on his haunches.

"No, Joseph, hold on. That's no way to behave. You come to see your friend Panayotti Helikos, because I'm sure you see me as your friend in spite of everything, so you've come to ask me for a favor, and what do I do? I say no! Why? You must think I'm saying no because I am working for your rival, right?"

"Isn't that the case?"

"Look, *ya habibi*. Business is business, that's true, all well and good, but a friend is not a thing you find just every day!" Helikos grabbed Hamdi-Ali's shoulders.

"You're telling me?" Joseph said and turned to leave. The sun was about to set on the horizon, and he blinked his tired eyes and asked himself what he was doing there. Panayotti caught up with him by the stables and grabbed his arm, pulling him inside.

"You don't understand me. You're my brother, Joseph. The fact that I work for that bloody Bedouin has nothing to do with it."

"Very nice." Joseph shook his head and tried once more, in spite of his growing exhaustion. "In that case, why won't you testify on my behalf in court?"

"I will, all right? I'll testify and say that, to the best of my knowledge, you're an honest man, and that I myself find it hard to believe that —"

"Hard to believe!"

"You want me to present him as a liar? Don't forget, old boy, he's my boss. *Kirio* Hamdi-Ali, you sure are putting me in an uncomfortable position. He'll destroy me, that Arab. I have a wife, Joseph, and children!"

"I'm not asking you to say Ahmed lied," Joseph said with a gloomy face. Shadows stretched along the empty track, climbing the white fences, falling down somewhere at the bottom of the stable wall. "I only asked that you tell them what happened at the club, when you and Toto and Sisso —"

"What?" Panayotti jumped up. This was too much. "You want me to tell the court that I was prepared to bribe you to help your son's horse lose the race?"

"It's true, isn't it?"

"But ... but it's illegal! Do you really expect me to

tell a thing like that to the entire world, and in a court of law, no less?" Panayotti burst out laughing, picked up a handful of straw and deposited it in Al Buraq's mouth. It was strange to see this horse, the animal at the root of all this commotion, eating so peacefully, oblivious to the goings-on of humans.

"You're taking your revenge on me," Joseph answered darkly. "You're getting back at me for not giving into you then. My integrity unnerved you. Now you won't testify on my behalf in court because you resent my integrity, my decency. You're all jealous of me, all of you." A smile began lighting Joseph's face, making him appear like a martyr confident that justice and God are on his side, taking pleasure in being burned at the stake.

Panayotti's face changed. "What integrity are you talking about?" he asked coolly.

"I'm an honest man, and that's what's upsetting you. That's why you won't testify that I'm innocent."

"How can I testify that you're innocent, how can I testify that you're *not* innocent? I don't know if you are innocent, and I don't know if you aren't. That's all there is to it!"

"You know I'd never do a thing like that!"

"How could I know that?"

"Because even when you made your ugly proposal, offering me sums of money that would corrupt the pope, I refused to cheat the spectators. Is that not proof enough?"

"Cheat the spectators? That's why you wouldn't take our bribe? That's news to me."

"Why else would I say no?" Joseph felt his face filling with blood. He barely held back from unleashing his anger on the small Greek man with the mongoose face.

Panayotti gave him a quick, ridiculing look, and began a merciless verbal assault: "You can't stand to see your son lose. *That's* the truth. On that blessed day when my Arab devil won, you were devastated. You can't watch your David come in second. That's your illness, that's your obsession, damn it. Is it any wonder that you drugged Al Buraq, too? If he could only talk, he would have told everyone. How you came to him at night, syringe in hand! All so that your son could win, all so that your Jewish papa's boy could win!"

Panayotti stopped for a moment to catch his breath. To Joseph, everything sounded abstract and unreal. "You want me to testify in court? You want me to tell them you're a raving fanatic, you have no true sportsmanship? That you're a sore loser? That you'd do anything for your son to win, even provide him with prostitutes? You think people don't know about that?"

These words pierced Hamdi-Ali's heart like a poisoned arrow and he cursed the thought of that Maltese waiter. One more so-called friend who sold me out for greed!

"Maybe you've been drugging the boy, too? To give him extra stamina? What wouldn't you do to win … always to win! Always! Always! Always!"

Joseph stood before him, unmoving, each word a sledgehammer. It wasn't very long ago that he'd almost strangled Ahmed Al-Tal'ooni. Why not do the same to this man here? But he stood there paralyzed. He, Yusef Hamdi-Ali, the king, doesn't dare! Panayotti wouldn't have dreamed of speaking to him like this a few weeks ago. Had things really changed that much? How low has he sunk, for a nobody like Panayotti to feel he no longer needs to fear Joseph Hamdi-Ali?

Tears ran down Joseph's face. Real tears, warm and salty, like a woman's—oh, the shame! Joseph hadn't cried since he was a child. He didn't even cry when Leila died, and now he was crying. He almost wanted to laugh at himself.

Panayotti was filled with pity but also with glee. He was seeing before him the downfall of the king of the racetrack. Not knowing what else to do, he walked away.

Joseph did not approach Toto and Sisso to persuade them to testify on his behalf. Suddenly it was all so unimportant, silly and sad, and he, he was the saddest of them all. There he was, naked to the world, and laughing. Laughing. He'd accepted the worst. He would be found guilty! Prison? A fine? A conviction would mean the end of his career. Then he realized. The end of his career meant …

This might have been when the idea first occurred to him.

At home, the heat and the suffocation were unbearable. The night was heavy and dead. He went out into the street, wearing only an undershirt, no fez, just like that, as if fleeing, but walking very slowly. His feet led him to the track. There was no one there but the guard, who knew him and let him in.

He walked into the fenced off area, like a veteran fighter returning to the battlefield.

He knew he'd lost the race, but he didn't care. He tried to conjure a memory of Leila, but she seemed to have foresaken him as well. He despised himself, hated his old body, his weakness, this burden on his shoulders—the family. He hated himself for having cried that day, and the more he hated himself, the more he pitied himself and the more he cried, without restraint, like the frightening symptom of some malignant disease. At first you don't take it too seriously, brushing it aside, thinking everything will be all right. But when the symptom appears a second time … and Joseph cried and cried. Along with his tears, the great distress that had been building up in him also came pouring out, and he felt relief. He was ready to live again. He regretted only that his body was so old.

Walking slowly, he stepped out of the gate and paced the sidewalk along Rue Delta, toward the sea.

37. Blanche

Joseph Hamdi-Ali was acquitted.

"Innocent for lack of evidence," said the honorable

judge. Joseph's attorney shook his hand with satisfaction and said, "We've sweated a lot, but you see, we got results, *al-hamdul-Illah!*"

His wife and eldest son were among the cheering crowd. They hugged him lovingly, and David said he felt like he'd just woken up from a bad dream, and that a celebration was in order.

Joseph was embarrassed. His mind was bothered by the lack of clarity in the term "innocent for lack of evidence." Well, is he innocent or not? Innocent, *but* ... does that mean he's guilty, God forbid? It was neither here nor there. Joseph raised his eyes to the heavens and smiled—up there, can one also be innocent for lack of evidence? And he, who'd been prepared for the worst, even for imprisonment, he who'd hoped and prayed for a full acquittal, for the clearing of his name, was suddenly finding himself drowning in a swamp of legal jargon. Only a full clearing of his name would have lessened the suspicion gnawing at his heart: that he'd been made a pawn of God and men.

David made a reservation at the Auberge Bleue, a pleasant club with a homey feel, where the performances featured both professionals and amateurs. Victor was ecstatic when he heard the entire family was going out together. When Joseph saw the happiness in his young son's eyes, he felt pity for the child, as if he'd finally been able to see the little outcast, who lived his life barely regarded. No one had meant to reject him, and yet it was as if he had been born an outsider, separate and pushed away, perhaps ... perhaps just like himself! He noted the sharp features, the long, slim neck, that twisted smile that seemed to be marking his own lips now, and he felt his insides yearning for this little man, his heart souring with compassion. Maybe this was his son, *his* kind of son, and he never knew it? Was it too late? At first Joseph thought of canceling the outing to the club, but Victor's joy changed his mind. Was he wrong about his fate? Maybe what he'd lost on the racetrack he would now find in the human race, in the family he'd neglected for so many years …

An intimate band played a quiet tango, drawing several couples onto the dance floor. David danced with his mother. Joseph remained alone at the table. Not alone, exactly—with Victor. As ever, fate leaves him alone with this strange boy who calls him Papa, and each time he wonders if he really means it. What he wouldn't give to start a conversation with this creature, his own flesh, growing wild, wandering free and lonely through the maze of adolescence. But what would he tell him? Would they talk about horses? Does the boy even care about horses? Maybe he should tell him about himself, about his childhood and youth in Turkey? But one cannot just open with these things with no apparent reason, and he craved so badly a conversation with his son. He began: "You … you want some *gelata*?"

The boy nodded. In the end, he's nothing but a child, Joseph thought with pleasure and relief. He signaled to the waiter. "*Garçon!*"

A waiter appeared immediately, as if sprouting from the parquet floor.

"Ice cream!" Joseph ordered jubilantly.

"Ice cream," the waiter confirmed.

"A mountain of *gelata*," Joseph added, laughing wholeheartedly. His son laughed, too. How easy, really; how easy it is to be a father.

Colorful heaps of ice cream arrived in a goblet. Victor stared at the mound, emitting sounds of glee and garnering glances from the nearby tables, though neither he nor his father paid any mind. Joseph wouldn't miss this moment because of a few dirty looks from people who might never have known and never would know true happiness. He rested his chin in his hand and watched his son dig in.

"You're spoiling him!" Emilie said reproachfully. A bit

breathless from the dance, she walked over to the table, a virginal blush adorning her cheeks.

"I'm spoiling him?" Joseph asked cheerfully. "You bet I am! I certainly am spoiling him! You want another?" he asked Victor.

"Yes, I do!"

"No, you don't!" David intervened.

"It's bad for him," Emilie interjected meekly.

"Nonsense!" Joseph determined. "*Garçon!* Another dish, a heap of gelata. And whipped cream ... Whipped cream, Victor?"

Victor nodded excitedly.

"And whipped cream! Lots and lots of whipped cream!"

Emilie tried to dissuade him once more, but to no avail.

"Let them talk," he told his son, winking at him.

"*Madame Hamdi-Ali. Monsieur Hamdi-Ali. David. Le petit Victor! Bonjour,*" a voice said behind them as Victor ravenously polished off his second helping of ice cream. They turned to the voice and saw Raphael, Aunt Tovula's son, and on his arm a young, smiling woman, her eyes projecting modesty.

"Raphael!" David called happily. "Come, join us!" He dragged a chair from a nearby table and signaled to the waiter to bring over one more.

"Please meet Blanche ... my fiancée."

"Congratulations! When's the happy day?"

"September. And then ... we're going away."

"Away? Where to?"

Raphael looked around him, then whispered, "Palestine."

"God be with you," Emilie wished them and sighed lightly.

"Thank you, thank you. We'll definitely need His help over there," Blanche said, laughing nervously.

"Don't worry, we'll join you soon," David said with a

giggle. It was obvious he had no intention of acting on this promise.

"Don't do any such nonsense, don't be foolish," Blanche said, and added hoarsely, "like us."

Then she fixed her green eyes on Raphael, who lowered his gaze and cleared his throat, leaned in and whispered, "We don't have a choice. I might be blacklisted because of my father, may he rest in peace, who lived in Palestine."

"He *might* be, and Raphael won't take any chances."

Slight embarrassment. The Hamdi-Alis had been entirely immersed in their own hardships, and here they were exposed to the most private world of others, without asking for it.

Suddenly Joseph called out, "We must drink in honor of this happy occasion. You're young! Palestine needs young people. God bless you, *à la vôtre*!"

They all looked at him, shocked, and Raphael turned around, afraid that someone might have heard the patriotic Zionism that had overcome the old man.

"We'd better drink to something else, something more important," Blanche said.

Raphael looked at her with worry. Who knew what this woman might say. He'd already noticed her tendency to humiliate him in public, when he couldn't properly defend himself. Robby's grandmother had warned against this daughter of Corfu. She would say, as if announcing a verdict, "There's nothing to be done. *C'est l'amour!*" Then she'd sigh for her nephew's fate and tell anyone who was willing to listen, "He's going to have some bitter times with her."

"More important?" Joseph wondered. "What could be more important than marriage? What could be more fateful than a journey?" He tried his best to be sociable. He even seemed to to have overcome some of his natural shyness, looking at Raphael's bride with brazen eyes.

"We heard you were acquitted. It was even in the newspaper," Blanche whispered hoarsely. Her words stung, and Joseph's smile faded away.

"In the newspaper?" Emilie asked.

"In the newspaper."

"Acquitted, *ma chère* Blanche, acquitted, but not innocent." Joseph winked with a bizarre mischievousness and leaned closer to the young woman. An intoxicating whiff of youth and cosmetics rose from her décolletage, making the old man feel slightly awkward. He watched her as if *she* were his real judge. Blanche shot him her enchanting smile, a wondrous blend: arrogance and control mixed with modesty and submissiveness. She fixed her mysterious smile on him and said nothing. The old man was left hanging, wanting to hear more, but she stayed silent. When her silence persisted he leaned closer and whispered in a plaintive, tired tone, as if asking to rest his head on her bosom: "Acquitted, but not innocent."

"Innocent?" Raphael rumbled. "You want someone else to decide for you whether or not you're innocent? You know what you are, and that's the only thing that matters."

"Maybe that's the only thing that matters," Joseph muttered at the interruption and stared back at the pretty fiancée. "But what matters doesn't matter here. Sometimes, what doesn't matter, matters!"

"I have no idea what you're talking about," Raphael said, as if Joseph had been talking to him.

"I do," said Blanche. "Would you like to ask me to dance, Mr. Hamdi-Ali?"

Silence.

"He can't d—" David began, but his father waved him off, stood up, took the young woman in his arms and danced. Raphael felt a deep hatred for the man, and Emilie smiled at him empathetically, as if to say, When you're my age you'll have more tolerance for this kind of thing.

"Raphaelo! Raphaelo! Raphaelo!"

The host announced, "I see him, in our audience, our friend Raphaelo with the angelic voice! Such a bashful tenor! It is our custom here at the Auberge Bleue to showcase talent from the audience, and so I truly hope Raphael Vital will be willing to sing a few songs from his repertoire, the songs of Andalusia."

Applause. The patrons all knew Raphael, or as they lovingly called him, Raphaelo. His voice had a rugged intensity and sensitivity. All the ladies shed a tear as he began singing the songs of España, the gentlemen awkwardly cleared their throats. Only Blanche sat there, shooting quizzical green arrows from her eyes to his. Never before had Raphael sung the suffering of the toreador captivated by the beautiful gypsy as emphatically as he did that day. Applause shook the walls. He smiled graciously at the audience, but looked at Blanche with concern. What does he care about the excitement of this audience if he doesn't have the support of his future wife? Blanche ran to him, kissed him in front of everybody and announced, "Raphaelo and I are getting married. *À la vôtre!*"

Everyone cheered, and Raphael looked at his fiancée gratefully.

38. To Die

Victor lay in bed, feverish, moaning, complaining, his stomach in knots. From time to time, he flew down the hallway to the bathroom; everyone hoped he made it there in time. For three days and three nights, there was a volcano in his stomach. The doctor came and wrote various prescriptions but the malady seemed to dance to the beat of its own rebellious drum.

Joseph stood at his son's side like a punished child. When Victor ran to the bathroom, Joseph ran after him, hoping he could help him, and thus repent for his sin. Ever forgiving, patient Emilie stared at her husband accusingly. Who gives a child a gallon of ice cream? And what if it was spoiled or poisoned, and who knows, the child could have ... God forbid ... she didn't dare complete the thought. But thoughts such as these had become harder to suppress ever since the cholera epidemic a few years back. She blamed herself, too. She should have made them stop after the first bowl.

Joseph walked out of the apartment. His wife ran to the balcony to follow him with her eyes; she didn't dare call after him to ask where he was going. She knew this did not bode well. Joseph quickly disappeared up the street.

An hour went by. The eruptions became less frequent. The child even managed to sleep for a while. His mother stood at his side, watching his face as it twisted with pain from time to time, and felt a surge of love for this boy. She swore that if he recovered, she'd give him much more attention than in the past. David was all grown up and would soon marry, and his wife would be there to take care of him. He won't want her, Emilie, with them anyway. Such is the way of the world. And this little one, who would he have left, other than her? And his father, she quickly added with alarm.

When Victor awoke there was a large, curious package at his side. He looked around quizzically and saw everyone surrounding him, smiling and gesturing for him to open the package. Quickly and enthusiastically, Victor began fussing with the ribbons and wrapping paper, finally removing the lid of the box and revealing the great wonder to one and all.

It truly was a wonder. Even Robby couldn't believe his eyes. He'd never seen anything like it.

Purring with joy, Victor hopped around on the rug like an excited monkey, not allowing anyone to come close. Victor made a special point of keeping Robby,

Salem, Thérèse and Juliette away, for the adults posed no real threat to the shiny toy sprawled over the rug.

Train cars scampered over shiny metal tracks with something between a rattle and a hum, passed through artificial tunnels, stopped at stations and intersections with red lights, attached themselves to locomotives, detached again, returned to their starting point, and embarked all over again, in mesmerizing circuitry. An imported train set, electric-powered, a world in and of itself. The user, the child, need only find a socket, flip the switch, and the busy system would come to life. Victor was ecstatic. His food poisoning faded into the background.

"Tell them! Tell them how much it cost!" Victor called out to his father.

Joseph looked at his son with pleasure and embarrassment. "Twenty. Twenty pounds."

And they all repeated with amazement: "Twenty pounds!"

Salem the servant stood in the corner and thought, how many times does two pounds eighty—Robby's father added thirty piasters to his monthly salary, despite Grandma's protests—how many times does that sum go into twenty pounds? He thought and thought, and when he couldn't calculate the answer, he concluded that if he could have done such math by himself, he would already be earning twenty pounds per month ... but ... seven! Seven was the answer. Two pounds eighty goes into twenty seven times, seven times his salary! Salem was proud to have solved the problem so quickly, but when the reality of the numbers sank in, his humiliation was overpowering. Salem was practical, a realist, like most other servants he knew. The fact that the world contained masters and servants was perceived by him as the moral foundation of a normal society, the way of the world, just like rising sun and the flow of the Nile. Nevertheless, there it was: a toy cost more than he earned in seven months? Would he ever be able to buy such a toy for his own son? Would his son end up a servant, just like him? His grandson?

Victor grabbed his father's neck once more and kissed his cheek. His father stood there, exhilarated, as if having achieved some spectacular feat. All the children were envious of his son, the little outcast. Just then Claude, the bespectacled mama's boy with the newsboy cap, appeared. He saw the train and begged Victor to let him play with it, but Victor wouldn't. Joseph caressed his happy son with his eyes, and suddenly, once again, but this time—how shameful it was!—in front of everyone, even the children and the servant and the two Coptic girls, tears burst from his eyes. The children stared at the crying old man and couldn't figure out what was happening. No one dared say a word.

Victor stopped his convulsions of joy and stood silently in front of his father. Then he jumped up at him once more and screeched, "You're the best father in the world. The best!"

Joseph wanted to die.

As simple as that, to die. His son was hanging on his neck, shouting into his ear that he was the best father in the world, and at that very moment Joseph felt that he wanted to die. Not for shame at having shed tears in spite of himself, not for rage at the things that had befallen him in recent days, not for desperation at the downfall of his career, not for disappointment in himself and his eldest son and his withering body, not for any clear, known reason. Just to die. For no reason at all. To cease …

Then, again for no clear or known reason, the train cars began changing directions, crashing into each other, making terrible noises, running off the tracks … running off the tracks … running off the tracks …

A short circuit ignited a white flash of light in the dimness of the hall, and the entire system shut down and died. In an instant, the complex web of trains turned into a heap of junk.

39. I'll Pray For You

Joseph was acquitted in the court of law, but not on the racetrack. Al-Tal'ooni was now the hero of the track, a national symbol. His wind-swept face, his deep, throaty voice, his unrestrained existence awoke deep yearning in a mob oppressed by an indifferent king who was surrounded by corrupt advisers, leaning on a crumbling empire, yearning for days of power and heroism in the free air of the scorching desert. Ishmael shall live on his sword! No more of Farouk's stockpiling, his paunch, his European suits, his fez and beads, his impotency. Al-Tal'ooni reminded the public of the days when Muhammad rode from Mecca to Medina and initiated a new calendar, of the days when Omar and Abu Bakr excited the imaginations of believers with the cry, "*Din Muhammad bi'l seif*— the law of Muhammad will be enforced with the sword!"

Al-Tal'ooni ruled the track, and his name resounded beyond the white fences and green grass of the Sporting Club.

Joseph didn't return to the track, despite his wife's and son's pleas. He knew he did not belong there anymore. You go, he told David. You go and take hold of your career, without your father's help, liberated from that dark shadow I cast around myself. Joseph snickered. Go, *ya ibni*, go... but he never believed his cowardly boy would go on his own.

David went. He trained alone, his Arab groom at his side. He slowly regained his previous form after a three-week break. He registered for the Sunday race, the final one that marked the end of the season in Alexandria.

"I'll participate in the final race," David said.

"The final race," Joseph repeated, his eyes glowing.

"I'll break that Arab," David said, enraged. "The whole world will know that the Hamdi-Ali name is the greatest of all!"

Joseph was happy. The zeal in his son's eyes—this is the boy he'd hoped for, this ambition, this determination. He could finally pass the torch in this inter-generational relay. He closed his eyes and said gravely, "I'll pray for you."

"You'll what?"

"I'll pray to our God that you win," said Joseph. "At the synagogue. I'll say ... I can't remember the words from the last time that ..." He went quiet. His conversion was an untouchable subject in the Hamdi-Ali family. They were all to pretend that Joseph had been born Jewish. He'd never come so close, dangerously close to stepping out of bounds, but he held his tongue just in time. Especially since little Victor knew nothing of the matter. That's what they thought, anyway, in fact, there was nothing Victor didn't know. "Still, I'll pray," he said, squeezed David's shoulder, sighed and stood up.

40. HAKHAM FERRERA

Rabbi Ferrera, in a fez and with a goatee, sat on the balcony sipping coffee with his eyes almost shut. In the tradition of Sephardic rabbis, he was known as "Hakham Ferrera"—"Ferrera the Wise." He fiddled with his prayer beads, and when his lips weren't touching the cup, they moved in a ceaseless mumble—the Psalms?—and his large Adam's apple, poking out of a thin, slightly twisted throat, went back and forth like a piston.

"Who's he waiting for over there, like a bird on a branch?" Madame Marika asked.

"You won't believe it: he's waiting for Joseph Hamdi-Ali," Robby's grandma whispered.

"Joseph Hamdi-Ali with Hakham Ferrera? Tsk tsk tsk. Now that's something!"

"And where is Monsieur Hamdi-Ali?" asked Alice, all

atwitter for the early Saturday game (she told Isidore she was going to visit a sick friend).

"Went downstairs for a newspaper," said Grandma, then added the startling news: "David's going to ride in the race tomorrow. Joseph's getting a paper to see what the betting situation is. He'll be right back." Not that she knew for certain what Joseph was reading in the paper about the race, and what the "betting situation" meant exactly, but she pretended to be fully informed.

"Why didn't he send the servant?" wondered Madame Marika.

"Joseph Hamdi-Ali goes to get the paper himself each morning."

"Those people from Cairo are strange!"

The ladies shook their heads and went to greet the rabbi. The wise man jumped up on his feet to honor *ces dames*, all smiles, and in his lyrical, chivalrous French, which contained some archaic vocabulary from past centuries, asked how their husbands were, and why they weren't also attending this friendly get-together, blessed by the sanctity of the Sabbath. The ladies admitted with downcast eyes that they'd convened to play cards.

"On a Saturday?" the rabbi said, shaking a reproachful finger at them. Then he sighed and continued: "Must you play cards on the Sabbath, too? It's forbidden."

He didn't expect an answer. Since he'd done his duty, he allowed himself to return to his coffee cup. He knew very well that his words made no impression on the ladies craving their card game. When his father, God have mercy on his soul, was the head rabbi of the community, people would be ashamed to be seen taking part in sacrilege. Times have changed, and Jews have changed. He was different from his father, too. He, who as a young man in his parents' house was more fanatical than his wise, tolerant father, had adjusted against his will, compromising, dragged after his flock, afraid he might lose it. He glanced at the women once more and sighed. In the meantime, Geena and Livia joined the group. The table was crowded. Including Robby's mother and grandmother, there were six women playing, while the maximum for each game was five. The hostesses decided to play *associées* instead, until a few more women showed up and they could fill a second table, with at least four in each game.

While they played, the rabbi finished his coffee, opened his eyes a slit and saw Robby. "Robbico, take this empty cup and tell your mother *yisalem ida*, bless her hands."

Robby took the cup, though he was angry at the rabbi for not summoning a servant for such an inferior task. While he was walking to the kitchen, the rabbi called him back again. "Robby, come here, Robby. *Viens ici*."

Robby returned to the old man.

"You want to be a *mezamer* at the synagogue?" he asked, fixing his brown and kindly smiling eyes on the boy.

"What's a mezamer?"

"A mezamer is a choir boy."

"And what do they sing?"

"Prayers, Psalms, things from the Bible." The rabbi knew how to speak to laymen.

"But I don't know the words. I don't even know any prayers."

"You'll learn. Come to the synagogue next Saturday and we'll teach you everything. But you know what? Wear nice Sabbath clothes. That's a *mitzvah*!"

Robby wanted to ask what a mitzvah was, but said instead: "But I can't sing."

"Do you think the other children can?" the wise Ferrera winked. "They don't know how to sing either. You move your lips in time. The main thing is to make them *think* you're singing. We need a lot of kids in the choir, you see? As many as possible. And maybe this will bring your parents to the synagogue. Here, have a piece of candy." He fished a sour candy wrapped in cellophane from his pocket.

Robby didn't like sour candy, but he didn't want to hurt the kind old man's feelings, especially since a career as a singer appealed to him in spite of his shyness. He could picture himself in a white suit and a loud red tie, a newsboy cap atop his head (because your head must be covered in the house of prayer), standing there, singing. Singing, yes. He was no longer ashamed, and promised himself to sing loud and clear, his voice rising above the rest. Nonetheless, one thing was certain—this would not draw his atheist father to the synagogue!

Joseph walked in with the newspaper under his arm. Seeing the rabbi, he hurried to put down the paper and walk over. "Rabbi, I'm sorry to make you wait."

"I was early, Yusef, *ya habibi*," the rabbi said good-naturedly. "Besides, I wasn't wasting my time. I was recruiting for our new choir. Here, Robby's going to join us as a mezamer."

Joseph turned to Robby, smiling. "Good boy, good boy."

It was one of the few times that Joseph Hamdi-Ali spoke to Robby. For a moment, the boy saw the old man's smiling eyes, two islands lost in a storm of wrinkles. Not the appeasing wrinkles of old age, those little ditches channeling intelligence and experience, but cracks in the heart of boiling lava, the geyser of tears about to erupt.

Joseph turned to the rabbi and said, "Rabbi, I thank you for agreeing to see me. I see you were already served coffee. I'll get straight to the point then." He shot Robby a quick look.

Robby, well-raised boy that he was, took the hint and left.

41. A Special Prayer

"I need your help, Rabbi," Joseph said gravely.

The rabbi nodded. It was his habit to help those in need, and so he was all the more attentive to Joseph Hamdi-Ali, the convert who contributed regularly to the community. He smiled and whispered, "How many years has it been, Yusef, my brother?"

Joseph did not respond. It was clear he didn't wish to touch upon this subject. He waited patiently.

The rabbi, oblivious, continued, "Thirty years, maybe more. Who can say? It goes by like a gust of wind." For a moment, Hakham Ferrera closed his eyes. A white room in Muharam Bey, Alexandria of the 1920s. His father, the rabbi, sitting on a low stool, flipping through the pages of the Talmud with quick, expert fingers, and the rapid movements of a professional swimmer. Once in a while he raises his eyes with a happy smile, removes his glasses and dives into the interpretation of a difficult topic. His son, having just stepped out of the realm of boyhood, drinks in his words thirstily.

At that moment, a skinny young man in a fez appears in the doorway. He turns to the old rabbi immediately and says in Turkish, "Sir Hakham, I want to become a Jew. How much?"

The shock on the old rabbi's face is slowly replaced with a merciful smile. "Before we discuss money, you must tell me why you want to become a Jew. Do you know how hard it is to be one?"

"I know," says the young man.

The excited rabbi's son jumps up and says, "Why do you need to even ask, *ya baba*? His eyes have obviously opened to the —"

His father glances at him and he quiets down immediately. Then the rabbi turns to the Muslim and says, "Well?"

The man answers without hesitation, "I love a Jewish girl and I want to marry her. Her parents would never let her marry a Muslim, that's why I want to be Jewish."

The romantic motive raises protest in the heart of the rabbi's son. "And where's the faith? The epiphany? All for a girl?"

Once more, his father looks at him admonishingly, and once more he quiets down. The old man asks, "What's your name, *ya ibni*?"

"Hamdi-Ali."

"Hamdi-Ali?"

"Yusef Hamdi-Ali."

"Listen, *ya* Yusef. We're a small people. We've always been a small people, because our God demands a lot of his believers, and not everyone is willing or able to meet these demands. Our religion is a difficult one, and not accepted by many. Our neighbors do not like us, and they'll like you even less. Because we, we were born Jewish, but you, one of their own, are turning your back on the religion of your ancestors ..." The rabbi shakes his head doubtfully. "Your neighbors, they won't like this one bit."

"Then we'll keep it a secret."

"A secret? How could you? You won't go to synagogue? You won't observe the mitzvot? You won't follow the customs of Israel?"

"Not the Judaism, we'll keep secret the ... the other religion."

"How is that possible? Does nobody know you here?"

"I'm new in this country. I got off the boat just yesterday."

"And your parents?"

"Dead."

"Dead?"

"As good as dead to me. And I'm the same to them."

Silence.

"I want to be Jewish," Joseph finally says.

"You want to marry a Jew, that's really what you want!" the rabbi's son spits.

"True, but nonetheless, I want to be Jewish."

The old rabbi shrugs and says, "Fine, if not on purpose then by accident. God willing, this will please Him. Where do you live?"

Joseph says nothing. He has no place to live. He certainly cannot stay with his fiancée's parents.

"The conversion process is long," says the rabbi. "Stay here, we have plenty of space." And he turns to his son with a smile. "As it says in the Torah, 'the foreigner sojourns among you.'"

"I'll pay you."

"Are you working?"

"No, but I ..."

"When you work, you can pay. The bed doesn't cost anything, and the food ..." the rabbi waved the thought away. "You don't look like you eat very much, anyway. My wife cooks for three and feeds at least half a dozen. We have two or three guests coming over for every meal. She won't even notice if she has one more mouth to feed." Then he laughed mischievously.

"I'll pay you. How much?"

"Have you got anything?"

"No."

"Then what are you proposing?"

"How much? I'll get a loan."

"Fine. One rial per month, room and board."

"And for the conversion."

"The conversion is a mitzvah."

"How much?"

"Donate to the community. To the poor. As you see fit."

After the conversion Hakham Ferrera senior married Joseph and Emilie according to the faith of Moses and Israel. Most of the guests, all on the bride's side, never guessed that Emilie was marrying a former Muslim. Only after years did the cloak of secrecy begin to fray. Suddenly, people began gossiping. How it was found out, no one could say. Among the Hamdi-Alis the matter was never to be spoken of, and none of the suspecting parties dared ask expressly if there was any truth to the rumor. And so the gossip remained hanging between uncertainty and the family's utter silence.

Perhaps this is why Joseph tried, after the marriage, and after leaving Hakham Ferrera's house, to minimize contact with the old rabbi and his son who succeeded him. They reminded him of the world he'd left behind and wished to erase. With almost cruel decisiveness he severed all ties with his parents, took no interest in their well-being, did not ask when they died or what became of his brothers. He kept only his name. In community records, a Yosef Ben-Abraham was registered, but he himself did not change his heavy Muslim name, the name which pulled him back to his roots. Why did he not change his name? Nobody knew, maybe not even he himself. Soon after they married, Emilie's father passed away and the young couple, along with the widow, moved to Cairo. Those days, Joseph began making a living riding horses, an activity favored by him since youth. And though the rabbis Ferrera—the father, may he rest in peace, and the son, may he live long and prosper, sitting with him now on the balcony—hadn't seen him more than three or four times in the many years that had gone by since, a check for two Egyptian pounds, a donation for the community's less fortunate, arrived at the community offices in Alexandria once a month, every month, for thirty years.

"I need your help," Joseph repeated. "It's a matter of life and death."

The rabbi's face turned serious. He saw the abysses open, the two wells of Yusef's eyes, their bottoms too deep to be seen. Yusef was not a joker. Nevertheless, when he thought of his words, the rabbi was embarrassed. A matter of life and death?

"The race is tomorrow," said Joseph. "Tomorrow—the final race. Then, there's a break. David will race. He must win. The way that David beat Goliath. Just like in the story, there is more to it than just those two. That's why David had to win then. And that's why David has to win now. A matter of life and death."

A pleasant breeze blew from the sea. The tumult of bathers sounded from afar: Muslims, Christians and Jews desecrating the Sabbath. On the street, cars honked hysterically. The entire city rumbled and roared; nevertheless a Sabbath serenity was felt all around. But the rabbi felt so distant. His late father might have understood immediately, but he thought of himself as a small, insubstantial man. Nothing but a *maître de cérémonies*, a sort of master of rituals of the synagogue; or, as he once said jokingly about himself, "the conductor of a choir of non-believers." Everything according to plan, a routine founded in the Jewish calendar, with no unexpected difficulties. But here was a Jew in trouble, and he didn't even know how to talk to him. "Why?" he asked.

"Why what?"

"Why is this a matter of life and death?"

Joseph held back his impatience. If the rabbi himself did not understand, how could he explain it? This was a matter one either understood immediately or never understood at all. Some people spent their entire life on the surface, in a closed, orderly world, never imagining what might be going on below, in the depths, in those twisting, dark tunnels where lost souls seek their way. A rabbi! A spiritual leader, and he doesn't know God, the devil, or death. Death! What could be more simple, more quotidian than death? How to explain this to him? Finally, he said with a sigh, "He's being put to a test, don't you see?"

"This isn't the first time he's participated in a race."

"Not him. Him. God. God Himself."

"What test?" Hakham Ferrera said awkwardly. He preferred not to bring God into this affair. The entire conversation seemed out of line, dangerous.

"I'd like you to say a special prayer, Rabbi," Joseph finally said.

"What do you mean, a special prayer?"

"What—what do I mean?" Joseph railed. "Today, at synagogue, a special prayer for my son to win the race tomorrow."

"A special prayer for a game of gambling?" the rabbi was outraged.

"This isn't about gambling, it's about—"

"Please, show me how this is a matter of life and death. Saving a Jewish soul, there is no bigger mitzvah, but it needs a foundation. You cannot bother God with mundane matters. It's as if ... as if ..." The rabbi's eyes bounced around and landed on the toy train in the darkness of the house, "as if you're pulling an emergency brake to stop a train midride—an act well-justified in a moment of danger, but entirely inappropriate when there is no peril." For some reason, Hakham Ferrera was not content with his own analogy. Later, he thought that his heart, at that moment, told him this was not a false alarm. He tortured himself for not having heeded his own intuition. But now, on the balcony, he asked himself what the nature of this distress might be. Yusef Hamdi-Ali had been acquitted, life had returned to its course. Next week the season in Alexandria would end, praised be the Lord, and everyone was already packing up to return to work, school, to the blessed routine that saves most people from purposeless wandering. What did he want? A matter of life and death? It was ridiculous, ridiculous! And nevertheless, Yusef Hamdi-Ali was not a man with a sense of humor. The rabbi squeezed Joseph's shoulder and assumed his most soothing voice: "What is it, what is it, *mon vieux*?"

Joseph couldn't explain such a simple and obvious thing: David wasn't David and Tal'ooni wasn't Tal'ooni. Neither of them was independent or autonomous. They were pawns in the hands of much mightier powers, fighting at all times and places and ways. Tomorrow they would battle on the track, and the winner would bring honor to his kin. Victory tomorrow would be decisive, final and complete. When he told the rabbi, "God is being put to the test," he had already gone too far. Such things need not be stated explicitly. Joseph felt a secret fear, one he'd never known before. His limbs shook, he could not subdue the storm raging inside him and he grew more and more tired. How could the rabbi not see that this was urgent? That the God of the Jews had to win? That if He didn't ... what would he himself do when faced with Him? With Allah the terrible, Allah who wreaks vengeance upon His enemies? It took place thirty years ago. It took place because of a woman. A woman he no longer loved. Love had faded, the deed remained. The deed that could not be repented. The day of judgment remained.

Hakham Ferrera pitied him. What was left of that energetic young man, that quiet, self-accepting man? He wanted to help but didn't know how. Saying a special prayer at the synagogue for a man to win a race? And what if some of the congregation members had placed bets on other horses? He'd be making a spectacle of himself and the synagogue. He and his institution were not properly respected these days anyhow, as in the days of his father. He himself was nothing but a sort of clown, an entertainer. He tried his best to please them all, and wasn't brave enough even to reprimand the women playing cards on Saturday in the adjacent room.

"I'll pay you," Joseph said impatiently.

The very same Hamdi-Ali he was thirty years ago! His solution for anything. "I'll pay!"

He wanted to issue a rebuke, but instead found himself

speaking sweetly through the dust of flattery, "You've been donating generously to the community for thirty years ..."

"Not to the community, I'll pay you!" Joseph said. "Straight into your pocket."

"Me?" Hakham Ferrera stood up. "Do you realize you're insulting me?"

Joseph wanted to slap the small, self-righteous man. He recalled another occasion, awhile ago, in that club, when he had rejected temptation. How much time had gone by? How many worlds had crumbled! Back then he could still look proudly in everyone's eyes, but today? What was he trying to do? Bribe a rabbi? Corrupt the entire world? He wanted to fall to his knees and beg for forgiveness. Instead he stood up and disappeared wordlessly into the darkness of the hall. In his move from the glaring brightness of the balcony to the darkness of the house he couldn't see a thing, and accidentally stepped on the toy train on the rug and trampled several cars.

The next day, looking back, the rabbi said in a trembling voice, "Perhaps I could have helped him. Perhaps. But I didn't."

42. The Street Lamplighter

The street lamplighter who rides through Rue Delta at dusk, kindling the gas lamps with his long lance topped by a small torch, returns once more along the same route late at night, while the street is deep in slumber. They say that with each lamp he extinguishes, one star goes out in the sky. When he completes his ride along the sidewalks and moves away down the boardwalk toward the east, his silhouette fades against the half-disc of the rising sun.

Just like that, every day, every week, every month, in all weather, for many years. One day electric lamps would be installed on Rue Delta, and then the lamplighter would disappear from the landscape, fading along with our forgotten childhood, which grows distant with every passing day.

The lamplighter saw a man lying on the sidewalk. A man sleeping on the sidewalk – not an uncommon sight in a Mediterranean city in the summer. The lamplighter shook his head and picked up whistling the Neapolitan tune that accompanied him through his route. He was about to continue to the next lamp when he noted the man's clothing. Fine, elegant European clothing.

It's a gentleman, he thought with surprise, not a beggar.

A European man sleeping on the street was not a sight frequently encountered by the lamplighter. During the war, British and Australian soldiers were everywhere in Alexandria. They got drunk at night and often couldn't find their way back to the barracks and fell asleep on the sidewalk until the sea breeze blew away the webs of intoxication from their eyes, or military police came to drag them away. "This *signore* must have gotten drunk too," the lamplighter thought. He wanted to get off his bike and check. Off his bike? Only at the end of the route! He was too lazy to come down. Instead, he poked the man with his long lance. The man did not budge. Eventually the lamplighter muttered an Italian curse and stepped onto the ground. He turned the man over on his back. There was a smile on his face. "Well sure, he's drunk." He leaned down and put his nose to the man's mouth, to check for the smell of alcohol, but couldn't detect a thing. It seemed the man wasn't breathing at all. Only then did he think that the man could be dead.

"A heart attack?" the Italian asked himself. "A man walks down the street and then … *basta! Finito!*" He began rummaging through the man's pockets to find his identification, but stopped. What if somebody walked by and thought he'd killed the old man to rob him? You try to be a good Christian and help another human being, even a dead one, and what do you get? Nothing but trouble!

He jumped back on his bicycle and rode away. He stopped to extinguish the next lamp and look back. A dark bundle lay beneath the previous lamp. The sidewalk was a little lighter back there.

When he reached the third lamp, the bundle had faded, swallowed into the blue grayness of the sidewalk. By the time he headed for the fourth lamp he'd forgotten the matter and returned to whistling that Neapolitan tune: "*O dolce Napoli, o sole beato…*"

And indeed, the sun's rays filtered down among the buildings along the street, slowly scattering golden dust on the face of the deceased. For a moment, it mischievously played upon the smile on the bluing lips. Joseph Hamdi-Ali had found peace.

43. *Oo Halasna!* And That's That!

Until the results of the autopsy were known, Emilie told whoever would listen that her husband had a heart of steel, that he never complained of pain, and that she couldn't understand how he, of all people, ended up having a heart attack on the sidewalk in the middle of the night.

The autopsy threw everything into upheaval. The doctors concluded that Joseph Hamdi-Ali fell onto the sidewalk from a height.

"Fell or jumped?"

It's difficult to recall who asked this question first. At any rate, in the next day's papers, the possibility of suicide was stated instead as fact.

Hakham Ferrera visited the widow and tried to console her as best he could. There were other esteemed visitors there, among them the Arab officer Nawas, friend of Robby's family. The rabbi sang Joseph's praises, calling him a better Jew than many who were born into the faith (suddenly everyone spoke freely of Joseph's conversion!), sighed and said that the community's poor would surely feel the absence of Hamdi-Ali. At this assertion, David quickly volunteered to continue in his father's footsteps and donate two pounds a month. Rabbi Ferrera went on and on but never mentioned the burial. How could he explain such a thing to the family? But then he couldn't ignore the feelings of an entire community either. Jewish law is unequivocal on this matter—not the matter of conversion, God forbid, but the matter of suicide.

Finally, David raised the subject, asking for the rabbi's advice about interment. "Papa ... will be released today from the ..." he swallowed, "morgue."

There was no getting around it. He had to say something. A man who sentenced himself to death cannot have a Jewish burial. Only outside the cemetery walls. But how to explain this?

The rabbi began speaking at length about burial laws and the needs of the deceased, talking in circles and exhausting his listeners, quoting technicalities from the scriptures, and while he fumbled and avoided any clear statements, it occurred to him to try to persuade the family to bury the man in Cairo. This way, responsibility would be transferred to the local Cairo rabbi, and he would be freed from this difficult decision. But David explained to the rabbi that his father had always wished to be buried in Alexandria. This is where he came when he left Turkey, this is where he converted to Judaism, this is where he married and this is where he wanted to be laid to his final rest.

The rabbi cleared his throat. The wishes of the deceased! What could one say against the explicit wishes of the deceased! Well, let it be, he thought and gathered his courage, and was about to ask the family members to speak with him privately when Emilie suddenly said,

"Did you see him when he was found?"

The rabbi was slightly confused. No, he hadn't seen him.

"He looked like an angel of the Lord," said Emilie.

The comparison made the wise man uneasy, but this was no time for chastising.

"Isn't it a miracle, *mon cher* Hakham, that Joseph's body remained intact after falling seven stories?"

"Intact?"

"It was as if he'd only lay down to rest for a moment before going on his way." She burst into tears once more. "God sent the angel Gabriel to help him get there …" This is what Joseph himself had said once, after Leila, in her first, wild days with him, almost threw him off her back.

"Like a parachute," Victor said, not meaning to be funny, but nevertheless receiving a cruel blow from David.

"Leave the little orphan alone," Emilie cried, protecting her young son. She clung to him and yelled in Arabic, "*Abuk mat, abuk rakh!*" Your father's dead, your father's gone. Mother and son wept in each other's arms.

True, Hamdi-Ali's body did appear whole. The autopsy later revealed that only the skin was untouched. Inside his body, the organs had turned to mush. The doctors were unable to explain it.

Officer Nawas asked again what the police had already inquired about that morning: Had the deceased left a note?

Emilie had found nothing, and neither had David or Victor.

"Suicide victims tend to explain their motives," Nawas said. "A man doesn't just jump off the seventh floor out of boredom, having not found a better way to amuse himself. He does this to prove something. Without a note, what is the point of the whole thing?"

"The officer's right," said the Hakham, standing up.

Why hadn't he thought of that himself? This gentile, with his mustache and uniform, solved in an instant the riddle that had been preoccupying him. Yosef Ben-Abraham could rest for eternity in a Jewish grave. "Joseph didn't kill himself, Emilie, I'm sure of it. He went up to the roof to get some fresh air … got dizzy … and … Adonai gives, and Adonai takes away, blessed is the name of the Lord. If he had planned on jumping, would he not leave a note?" He sat down, satisfied and turned to the officer. "*Mush keda, ya sidi?* Isn't it so, sir?"

Nawas confirmed the matter with a wide smile, glad to have his version accepted. His friend who was investigating the case would be happy to close the dossier.

"Can the officer make sure that the investigator in charge of this case sends an appropriate message to the press, especially the European press?" asked the rabbi. If even a tiny statement appeared in *Le Progrès Egyptien*, the paper read by his community, no one would be able to say he'd made an exception for his precious convert. It was a tragic accident, *Oo halasna*, and that's that!

Emilie almost smiled with relief.

44. RAIN

The tiny Topolino curled up, asleep, along the sidewalk. The royal family stood beside it. The entire household was bent over in sadness. Four had come there, but only three would leave. The little car would no longer be so cheerfully crowded as it raced down the Cairo-Alexandria road. There would be no more expectation tickling in their fingertips, the expectation of early summer. The sky was cloudy, leaning heavily on the flat roofs of the buildings. It was as if the city had been plagued with the early onset of old age, and a gray murkiness poured over its face. Emilie Hamdi-Ali, a former queen, was plopped over her son's arm like a tired old sack, hunched over, her life devoid of meaning. Few women in Egypt had a life of their own. Most of them lived the hopes and dreams of their husbands. They'd been trained since childhood to be trusty companions, shadows.

In the gray clouds, the sun looked like an exhausted, pale blotch, too tired to sketch shadows on the sidewalk. Objects seemed scattered pointlessly, with no forethought, like a collage in an illustrated magazine.

The preparations were carried out calmly, in utter silence. Salem carried suitcases and bundles with his usual lassitude, and Badri the doorman and his son did not make too much of an effort, since the young *Hawaga* Hamdi-Ali was not known to be very generous.

What surprise they all felt then, when at the end of the loading process, David gave each of the three men a whole rial. Salem thought: the Hawaga David is confused with grief. The doorman's son could not contain his pride. He'd never held such a sum of money in his hand. Twenty piasters! But his joy was short-lived. His father snatched away his reward, and when the child tried to protest, Badri slapped the back of his neck fiercely, and he fell to the sidewalk and burst out crying. Salem pitied the pathetic soul and fished one mil from his pocket to give to the child. He was proud to be able to give, like a true Hawaga. That Salem ... he was a special boy. Alert, clever, not too industrious and not too lazy either. Incredibly talented at picking up languages by ear (French, a bit of English and even Ladino), and most of all—self-sufficient, with a world of his own which no one else could enter. Had he been born in a different class, in a different time, he might have made it far. And perhaps he had made it after all? Maybe Salem was one of those whose horizons had been suddenly opened by the Officers' Revolution? For years, Robby wondered what became of the boy who grew up in his home with him.

Robby stood by the balcony railing as the small car went on its way, swallowed up beyond the bend in the road at the boardwalk. For a moment he looked at the gloomy, thickening sky, and felt his throat contract. Why was he working harder than ever today, in a sort of desperate fervor, to take down license plate numbers? He hurried to dip his pen in the ink well placed on the railing, and wrote, and wrote and wrote ... He'd missed only one car. Not bad.

Suddenly a drop landed on his head. He looked up once again, and was hit by another drop, straight in his eye. Then another on the tip of his nose. The first rain. Robby ran inside and announced all through the house, "It's raining! The rain is here!"

The notebook was left on the railing, and the rain splattered over the numbers, the water blurred the ink, blurred the shapes, erased everything.

A gust of wind blew the notebook off the railing, and the soggy mess fell to the ground.

The summer was washed off the city streets. Winter came to Alexandria.

Guys Like Me BY DOMINIQUE FABRE

Dominique Fabre, born in Paris and a life-long resident of the city, exposes the shadowy, anonymous lives of many who inhabit the French capital. In this quiet, subdued tale, a middle-aged office worker, divorced and alienated from his only son, meets up with two childhood friends who are similarly adrift. He's looking for a second act to his mournful life, seeking the harbor of love and a true connection with his son. Set in palpably real Paris streets that feel miles away from the City of Light, a stirring novel of regret and absence, yet not without a glimmer of hope.

I Called Him Necktie BY MILENA MICHIKO FLAŠAR

Twenty-year-old Taguchi Hiro has spent the last two years of his life living as a hikikomori—a shut-in who never leaves his room and has no human interaction—in his parents' home in Tokyo. As Hiro tentatively decides to reenter the world, he spends his days observing life from a park bench. Gradually he makes friends with Ohara Tetsu, a salaryman who has lost his job. The two discover in their sadness a common bond. This beautiful novel is moving, unforgettable, and full of surprises.

Who is Martha? BY MARJANA GAPONENKO

In this rollicking novel, 96-year-old ornithologist Luka Levadski foregoes treatment for lung cancer and moves from Ukraine to Vienna to make a grand exit in a luxury suite at the Hotel Imperial. He reflects on his past while indulging in Viennese cakes and savoring music in a gilded concert hall. Levadski was born in 1914, the same year that Martha—the last of the now-extinct passenger pigeons—died. Levadski himself has an acute sense of being the last of a species. This gloriously written tale mixes piquant wit with lofty musings about life, friendship, aging and death.

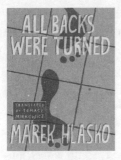

ALL BACKS WERE TURNED BY MAREK HLASKO

Two desperate friends—on the edge of the law—travel to the southern Israeli city of Eilat to find work. There, Dov Ben Dov, the handsome native Israeli with a reputation for causing trouble, and Israel, his sidekick, stay with Ben Dov's younger brother, Little Dov, who has enough trouble of his own. Local toughs are encroaching on Little Dov's business, and he enlists his older brother to drive them away. It doesn't help that a beautiful German widow is rooming next door. A story of passion, deception, violence, and betrayal, conveyed in hardboiled prose reminiscent of Hammett and Chandler.

KILLING AUNTIE BY ANDRZEJ BURSA

A young university student named Jurek, with no particular ambitions or talents, finds himself with nothing to do. After his doting aunt asks the young man to perform a small chore, he decides to kill her for no good reason other than, perhaps, boredom. This short comedic masterpiece combines elements of Dostoevsky, Sartre, Kafka, and Heller, coming together to produce an unforgettable tale of murder and—just maybe—redemption.

COCAINE BY PITIGRILLI

Paris in the 1920s—dizzy and decadent. Where a young man can make a fortune with his wits … unless he is led into temptation. Cocaine's dandified hero, Tito Arnaudi, invents lurid scandals and gruesome deaths, and sells these stories to the newspapers. But his own life becomes even more outrageous when he acquires three demanding mistresses. Elegant, witty and wicked, Pitigrilli's classic novel was first published in Italian in 1921 and retains its venom even today.

SOME DAY BY SHEMI ZARHIN

On the shores of Israel's Sea of Galilee lies the city of Tiberias, a place bursting with sexuality and longing for love. The air is saturated with smells of cooking and passion. *Some Day* is a gripping family saga, a sensual and emotional feast that plays out over decades. This is an enchanting tale about tragic fates that disrupt families and break our hearts. Zarhin's hypnotic writing renders a painfully delicious vision of individual lives behind Israel's larger national story.

THE MISSING YEAR OF JUAN SALVATIERRA BY PEDRO MAIRAL

At the age of nine, Juan Salvatierra became mute following a horse riding accident. At twenty, he began secretly painting a series of canvases on which he detailed six decades of life in his village on Argentina's frontier with Uruguay. After his death, his sons return to deal with their inheritance: a shed packed with rolls over two miles long. But an essential roll is missing. A search ensues that illuminates links between art and life, with past family secrets casting their shadows on the present.

THE GOOD LIFE ELSEWHERE BY VLADIMIR LORCHENKOV

The very funny—and very sad—story of a group of villagers and their tragicomic efforts to emigrate from Europe's most impoverished nation to Italy for work. An Orthodox priest is deserted by his wife for an art-dealing atheist; a mechanic redesigns his tractor for travel by air and sea; and thousands of villagers take to the road on a modern-day religious crusade to make it to the Italian Promised Land. A country where 25 percent of its population works abroad, remittances make up nearly 40 percent of GDP, and alcohol consumption per capita is the world's highest – Moldova surely has its problems. But, as Lorchenkov vividly shows, it's also a country whose residents don't give up easily.